I0817802

PINA COLADA POISON

Charlotte Gibson Mysteries #4

JASMINE WEBB

Chapter 1

I sprinted past an azure sign decorated with fruits and greenery, with pastel-pink lettering advertising that the farmer's market was on today in north Kihei. My eyes were fixed on my target: Anthony Chekov. Thief, womanizer, and—I assumed—man who had been a championship runner back in high school.

Why couldn't the guy I was after be more of a chess club kind of guy? Maybe missing a leg. He would have been *much* easier to catch, and it turned out I was *not* fit.

"I went on a hike like two months ago. Why am I so out of shape?" I panted to myself as Anthony darted into the market. It was very rustic, with wooden frames topped with canvas tents that led into a paradise of fresh fruits, vegetables, baked goods, and my personal favorite, passionfruit cream cheese.

Stunned shoppers jumped out of the way as Anthony sprinted past them, with me following hot on his heels. Okay, lukewarm on his heels. Suddenly, he slipped on the surface of small gray cobbles, stumbling for a second. He took a second to look back, his eyes widening when he saw I was still on his tail.

Maybe I wasn't doing as badly as I thought. Well, apart from the fact that my heart felt like it was about to explode and my legs were screaming at me to just chop them off and put them out of their misery.

Anthony grabbed a pineapple from one of the nearby stands, and hurled it in my direction. I ducked out of the way, and the pineapple hit the wall behind me with a thud while the stall's owner yelled at Anthony.

"Hey! That costs four dollars!" he shouted, but Anthony ignored him. He almost stumbled and fell against one of the stalls, using the wooden table to keep himself upright, and ran to the left.

"Someone stop him," I gasped in desperation, hoping that I'd get a little bit of help. It came in the form of one of the stall owners, who, as Anthony was running past, smacked him square in the face with a container of guacamole, the green goo splattering across Anthony's face as he let out a yell. It knocked him off-balance, and he fell to the floor, clawing at his eyes.

"What the hell, man?"

"You owe Pukalani four dollars," the man said, standing over Anthony with his hands on his hips. I took advantage by jumping onto Anthony and zip-tying his hands behind his back.

"You're under citizen's arrest until the cops get here. Don't think I didn't see you robbing that jewelry store down the street earlier. And I have the camera footage to prove it."

Suddenly, everyone in the farmer's market began to clap. I looked up, kind of embarrassed, as about a dozen people, a mix of tourists and locals, all happily cheered the capture of a criminal who was spitting out bits of avocado.

"Fresh guacamole!" the man who had stopped Anthony announced, grabbing another container from the box full of ice on which sat about a dozen tubs of the stuff. "Made this morning, right here in Kihei! Very good price. Stops criminals in their tracks!"

I had to admire the hustle.

"You want to get me a towel or something?" he spat at me.

"Not especially. Thanks for the help," I said to the shopkeeper as I dragged a scowling Anthony to his feet, ignoring the shooting pain in my arm. Who knew it took so long to get over a bullet wound?

The shopkeeper replied, "You're welcome. Too much crime in our neighborhoods these days. We have to stop it. It's the Hawaiian way."

"I agree. Anyway, let me buy some guacamole from you. Least I can do." I pulled a wad of cash out from my pocket and began counting out the bills, while keeping a close eye on Anthony, who was still trying to shake the bits of avocado sauce from his face.

"Really, lady? You're buying condiments right now?" Anthony muttered.

"That's a pretty judgemental attitude for a guy

who's going to spend the next ten years in Halawa," I replied.

Anthony kicked at the stones by his feet.

"And don't you even *think* about running away. Because the jewelry shop owner will have called the cops the instant you left, and I bet they're arriving on the scene right about now. If you run, they're going to Taser you—if you're lucky—and let me tell you, a vat of sauce to the face is a lot better than having thousands of volts of electricity running through your body."

"You're such a bitch," Anthony snapped. "Why were you even here?"

"The really funny part about this is that if you'd kept it in your pants, you might be running off with that jewelry you stole. But your wife, Charlene, she figured out what you were up to. You were going to work as a plumber every day, but you were cleaning pipes on the side too, and I'm not talking PVC. Well, Charlene hired me to prove what you were up to so that she could wipe the floor with you in the divorce proceedings. She wants full custody of the kids, and wants as much ammo as she can to get it. So, I've been on your tail for the last four days and nights. I know all about Arlene. And Heather. And Michelle. But little did I know you were going to go for Tiffany too. I didn't think you needed the cash enough to hold up a jewelry store."

Anthony scowled. "Heather was pressuring me. She wanted me to leave Charlene, but I wasn't going to.

Charlene's family has money. If I'm on my own, I've got nothing."

"Come on, nobody who's ever had a leak thinks plumbers are poor."

"Yeah, but it's not like the lifestyle I live with Charlene. Two cars. House in Wailea. Dinners at the Four Seasons. I can't do that on just a plumber's salary. Heather was pressuring me, so I thought I'd shut her up for a bit. Figured some nice jewelry would get the job done. And I knew old man Lehman down here runs minimal security during the day. Cameras, of course. And a panic button. But the idiot's a pacifist. Doesn't carry a gun. I figured it'd be easy as anything to just get a couple things and disappear. Until you came and messed it up."

"Poor you, life is so rough for the oppressed thief these days."

Anthony scowled at me as I dragged him back toward the entrance of the market, past curious shoppers. Outside, the red and blue lights of police cruisers cut through the white light of the day.

"Time to go. Off to jail," I said. I exited the building, and my eyes immediately landed on Detective Jake Llewelyn. Perfect. I strutted toward him, an annoyed and guacamole-covered Anthony next to me.

This was a scene right out of the end of an episode of CSI. I could see it in slow-motion in my head. I was doing the perp-walk, bringing Anthony to Jake on a silver platter. Sunglasses on my face, my brown hair glistening in the sun as the waves bounced up and down, the confidence from having caught my man giving me a strut in my step.

I was sure I looked hotter than hell right now.

I walked right up to Jake, bringing Anthony along with me. Now, all I had to do to finish the scene was make a witty comment.

Before I had a chance to say anything though, Jake squinted at my face. "Is that guacamole on your cheek?"

Cue the record-scratching sound. There went my cool-looking slow-mo. I looked like someone who went too hard at the Mexican restaurant. Of course I did.

I scowled, reached up to my cheek, and wiped away the offending goo. "Well, I brought you a perp." It was a good thing I didn't need a pithy remark anymore; I had nothing anyway.

Jake spun Anthony around and cuffed him. "You avo right to remain silent," he said with a grin, and I laughed at the pun. Damn it. Why did Jake have to have the clever phrase?

"Okay, I'm actually going to redo the Miranda warning just in case. I don't want to have to explain to a judge why the case got thrown out on a technicality because I couldn't resist a good pun. Let me just put this guy in the car, and I'll be back to take your statement."

"He's all yours."

I watched as Jake led Anthony off toward one of the police cruisers while he reread the man his rights. I totally wasn't checking out his butt.

A couple minutes later, Jake returned, which had

given me just enough time to use my phone's front camera to make sure I didn't have any more guacamole on my face. Just the container I'd bought in my other hand.

"What are you doing here, anyway?" I blurted out, and he raised a single eyebrow skyward.

"My job? I was going to ask you the same question."

"Also my job."

"Really? It was sheer luck that you ended up stumbling upon a brazen daylight robbery?"

"Mostly. Technically, I had been watching Anthony. His wife wanted proof of his affairs, so I've been following him for the last four days. I didn't realize Anthony Chekov was a thief as well as an adulterer."

"He had a gun. You could have been killed."

"He dumped the gun in the trash can over there on his way out," I said with a nod in the direction of the receptacle in question. "There was no real risk. And as you can see, I came out slightly less covered in guacamole than he did. I consider that a win."

Despite himself, Jake laughed. "Fine. He looks like the world's lamest version of the Hulk. Can you give me a rundown of everything that happened? I'll type it up when I get to the station."

Jake pulled out his phone and turned on the recording app, while I recounted everything that had led to me chasing Anthony Chekov through the market. When I was finished, Jake turned off the recording.

"I suppose I should just be glad you didn't get

Tasered this time," Jake said when I was finished. "Even your normal jobs end up going weird."

"I think the words you're looking for are 'thank you,'" I replied. "After all, I handed you a criminal on a silver platter today. Instead of whining about how the Maui Police are incapable of stopping crime, the papers are going to have to go on about how the Maui Police did a great job arresting the criminal only moments after the brazen daylight robbery."

"That's a good point. And you did see him ditch the gun before going after him. I guess I can't fault you for being in the right place at the wrong time."

"That's right," I said smugly, crossing my arms in front of me. "You just wish you were this lucky."

"I'm just glad you're as lucky as you are. You've earned your fee on this one, anyway. Anthony Chekov is going to jail for a long time, so Charlene should have no problem with the divorce."

"I only wish he had stolen the jewelry *before* I had to spend half the night watching his bare ass through the window. It was so pale it was like watching the full moon. If the full moon was only out for two minutes a night."

Jake snorted. "That's way more information than I ever wanted to know."

"Hey, you got off easy. I had to look at it. And take pictures. I think my camera committed suicide in protest."

"I tried to warn you this wasn't the most glamorous job."

"You did not. You tried to warn me that I was going

to end up a corpse on the beach, and that hasn't happened."

"Thankfully. Anyway, I'm sure you've got a lot more pictures of full moons in your future," Jake said with a grin. "For now, I'm going to go book Anthony. I'll be in touch. My bet is his lawyer convinces him to go for a deal."

"I'll see you around."

"Hopefully just at the apartment building, and not at crime scenes."

"You're welcome," I called after Jake's retreating figure. I turned, rolling my eyes, thinking Jake was probably doing the same. I was hungry. Maybe I should go back into the market and get a tub of passionfruit cream cheese. After all, I'd earned it.

Chapter 2

Two hours later, I was driving Dot and Rosie, two of my best friends in the world, to Olivia's garage to pick up Rosie's SUV. Finally freed from the prison that was the Maui Police Department's evidence lot after nearly two months, Rosie's vehicle had come back, riddled with bullet holes. Luckily, most of them had hit the frame of her ten-year-old CR-V, and only one bullet had gone through my arm.

After surgery, physical therapy, and a *lot* of painkillers, my arm was mostly back to normal. It still hurt like a mofo if I raised my arm above my head, or if I twisted it weird, but in my day-to-day life, I could get along just fine.

Besides, I was now an expert at scooping ice cream left-handed.

Once Rosie had gotten her car back, while Dot thought she should keep the bullet holes, "so everyone in the parking lot knows not to mess with you," Rosie decided to get them fixed. Hence the ride to Olivia's place to pick it up.

Olivia had sold me Queenie, my black-and-neon-blue Jeep Wrangler that was basically the same vintage as I was, and that I loved more than most people on the planet. The child of hippies, Olivia lived and worked out of a shabby old bungalow in Waikapu with her Rottweiler, Egg McMuffin—he went by Egg. She was also an absolute genius with cars.

As I pulled into the driveway, the car's tires slowly crunching over the bits of gravel, Olivia looked up from the open garage in front of me. There was Rosie's CR-V, looking good as new. Well, as new as a ten-year-old SUV that had been showered by bullets could look, anyway. She grinned and waved, wiping her brow, leaving a smear of grease across her forehead.

I jumped out of the car and was met with an enthusiastic bark. Egg came running out from the side of the house, tennis ball in his mouth, drool spraying in every direction, like a lawn sprinkler in the summertime.

When he reached me, he skidded to a stop, dropped the ball at my feet, and panted excitedly.

"Hey, boy," I said with a grin, grabbing the ball and hurling it underhand across the yard as hard as I could. Egg took off after it, four legs lumbering along while his tongue flapped along outside his mouth.

"She's all ready for you," Olivia said, wiping her hands on a rag as she came out to meet Rosie and Dot. "Just a quick body fix. Though I did notice that when you've got four-wheel drive engaged, there was a bit of creaking coming from the rear differential, and when I turned the car, it would vibrate a bit. That's caused by contaminants in the rear diff oil, which causes traction of the internal parts. I replaced the oil to fix that up for you."

"Well, thank you very much," Rosie said appreciatively. "Charlie did say you were the best."

"Hey, better me than some dude who'll charge you a couple hundred bucks for it, and probably try to sell you a new transmission while he's at it," Olivia replied with a grin. "This baby's in great shape overall. You must take excellent care of it."

"She does," Dot replied. "Almost always drives the speed limit. Only gets shot at occasionally."

I snorted a laugh while Egg came running back with the ball. I launched it to the other side of the yard for him again, and he scampered after it once more.

"Luckily, this is only the second time I've had to deal with bullet holes in my vehicle, and I must say you have done a much better job than the person who fixed it the first time."

"Wait, what was the first time?" I asked, but Rosie simply replied with an enigmatic smile.

"Should you find yourself in need of more patching up in the future, you know where to find me," Olivia said with a laugh as she handed Rosie an invoice. "By the way, I heard there was some kerfuffle down in Kihei this morning. Someone robbed one of the jewelry stores down on South Kihei Road."

I grinned. "Yeah, I'm the one who took care of it."

Olivia looked impressed. "Damn. Well, remind me not to get in your way in the future."

"I'm pretty good at what I do. If you know anybody looking for a private investigator, I'm always looking for new clients." It still felt a bit strange, advertising my services like that. It had been a couple of months, and I still wasn't used to it.

"I'll keep my ears open."

After a bit more casual conversation, and Egg getting the tennis ball thrown for him a few more times, the three of us headed home. Rosie was going straight to her place, and I lived closer to Dot, so she rode back with me in Queenie.

"You need to get yourself a custom stereo system in this thing," Dot said as we headed back down toward the highway, mashing the old plastic buttons.

"Why? I like the radio just fine."

"That's old-people talk. The radio sucks. Half the time you get ads. I want to listen to my Spotify on here."

"If you pay for a sound system, you can listen to Spotify in the car."

"I don't want it that badly," Dot grumbled. "Fine. The radio it is."

She leaned forward and began messing with the dials. "There's no good music on this thing," she grumbled.

"What do you listen to?" I asked, not daring to guess. With Dot, the answer could have been anything from Bach and Beethoven to Black Sabbath and Bon Jovi.

"Seventies British rock and eighties hair bands,"

Dot replied without missing a beat. Hey, I nailed it with Black Sabbath and Bon Jovi.

"Okay, well, I can't help with that, but I can tell you what channel has the top forty hits," I replied as Dot scanned past a country song while making a gagging noise.

"Breaking news, Hollywood superstar Marion Hennessey has been whisked away from the beachside patio at the Maui Diamond Resort, where a guest was found to be in medical distress."

Dot paused and raised her eyebrows. "Okay, this is more interesting than listening to *Kashmir* for the ten thousandth time. Tell me more, radio man."

The voice on the other end of the line continued, a tiny bit of static overriding the smooth newscaster's drone. "According to reports, Hennessey was at the restaurant enjoying drinks with a handful of friends here in Maui, where she regularly spends her holidays. After playing the role of Alicia Marquet in the 1984 flick *Pink Skies and Pretty Lies*, which filmed here on the island, Hennessey purchased an oceanfront home and has been spotted regularly at the hottest restaurants and clubs. There is no indication yet as to the relationship Hennessy had to the person in medical distress."

"Wow, thanks for the nothing report," I said, rolling my eyes. "Someone got sick at the resort, now here's a bunch of information about a celebrity who happened to be in the vicinity."

"Plus, the reporter's right. Marion Hennessey is on the island so often she practically lives here now. I don't blame her, either. If I had as much fame and money as she does, I'd be on the next plane out of LA. Sure, it has palm trees and the ocean, but that's where the similarities end."

"I've never been," I admitted.

"Well, it sucks," Dot said matter-of-factly. "The weather is nice, but everything smells like pee, you spend ninety percent of your life stuck in traffic, and everyone looks better than you."

I laughed. "Not a fan, then?"

"It's worse than Alaska, and that's saying something," Dot muttered. "No, I'm a Maui girl through and through. You could never get me off this island."

"Yeah. I'm starting to feel that way myself." I had always told myself I wouldn't come back to Maui, that it was too painful. But now that I had been back here for a while, it felt like home again. I loved being able to drive my open Jeep in March, the warm afternoon air whipping my hair around while the sun gleamed off the hood. I loved the slower pace of life here, and the Aloha spirit, which was alive and well for those who chose to embrace it.

"Anyway, I just like the idea of Marion Hennessey enjoying her time here. I've never met her myself, but everything I've heard makes her out to be a very nice person."

"She was here at Christmas," I said, nodding. "I saw an article about her. She left a thousand-dollar tip on a meal in Ka'anapali."

"I hadn't heard that, but yes, it sounds like the sort of thing she'd do. Well, I hope her friend is all right, whoever it is."

"Me too."

THE NEXT DAY, I WOKE UP AROUND NINE. LESLIE HAD managed to hire someone else to work with her at Aloha Ice Cream, which meant I was working fewer shifts, which was fine with me. Zoe was at work at the hospital, so I had the run of the place, and I decided to take Coco, my little golden retriever and dachshund mix, for a walk along the beach.

I was watching Coco as she ran along the beach, her little stomach grazing the sand as she hopped along, happily sniffing whatever came her way, when my phone began to ring. Checking the caller ID, I didn't recognize the number. Or the area code—323. It was probably one of those spam phone calls, telling me I owed back taxes and that the U.S. Marshals were going to come and arrest me if I didn't immediately pay them in iTunes gift cards and bitcoins—because as everyone knows those are the two currencies favored by the IRS—but I picked up anyway.

"Hello?"

"Hi, is this Charlotte Gibson?"

"Speaking."

"You were recommended to my client as a private investigator on this island, and she would like to hire you. Are you available to meet with her today?"

"Uh, sure," I replied, a little surprised. "Of course. Where and when would you like to meet?"

"Honolulu Coffee Company, the one in Wailea. In an hour. You can be there?"

"No problem," I replied.

"Good."

The woman on the other end of the line hung up, and I realized I didn't even know who she was, or the name of her client who I was supposed to meet with.

Some investigator I was.

"Come on, Coco," I called out to my dog, who was busy digging a hole, probably going after a crab under the sand. "Time to go home."

Coco sprinted toward me, and I clipped her leash back on to take her back to the apartment so I could get ready for my mystery meeting.

Chapter 3

I arrived at the Wailea Honolulu Coffee branch ten minutes early, so that whoever my potential new client was would have to find me instead of the other way around. Located in one of the most upscale malls on Maui—The Shops at Wailea—Honolulu Coffee was located in a small enclave. On one side was a Tiffany and Co. store, the other Prada, and directly across from it was Louis Vuitton.

I definitely wasn't in Kihei anymore.

Trying not to feel intimidated as I walked past the purses in the window that cost more than my monthly rent, I entered the coffee shop. Honolulu Coffee was made with coffee from Kona, on the island of Hawaii, and had quickly grown to not only be a staple on the islands but an international sensation.

The interior was so quintessentially Hawaiian I instantly relaxed a little bit. The walls were painted a bright lemon yellow, while half-moon aqua-colored awnings over the large windows broke up the space. Palm-frond-shaped fan blades spun above, creating a gentle breeze, and to the left were shelves upon shelves of roasted coffee in the signature forest-green bags, along with an assortment of mugs and other coffee paraphernalia adorned with Hawaiian motifs.

In front of me, the woman at the register smiled, her straight black hair pulled into a high, tight bun. "Hi there. How can I help you?"

My eyes moved to the menu board on the back wall, decorated with a woven wicker pattern. In the center, a large, glossy piece of wood featured the company logo.

"I'll have a Hawaiian iced latte, please," I said, handing the woman a few bills. A latte with coconut and macadamia flavor sounded like exactly the sort of drink I needed today.

I was pleased to find that despite being in a mall where the target demographic was one with far more disposable income than I had to offer, the coffee wasn't exorbitantly priced, and I made my way to the tables outside in the open air.

It was still early, and I found a free set of wood-framed outdoor chairs with enormous green upholstery and yellow cushions, a small wooden table in between them. A large square umbrella above blocked the heat of the sun, and I waited for my client to arrive.

This was one of the most luxurious places to shop on the island, and these seats certainly beat the normal wood-and-metal benches found in most outdoor malls.

I was facing the entrance to Honolulu Coffee,

thinking that whoever my client was, one of us would hopefully be able to spot the other. If not, well, they obviously had my phone number, and I was sure it would work out. A few moments later, my eyes widened in surprise and my heart began beating a little faster when none other than Marion Hennessey walked past the entrance to the coffee shop and made her way directly toward me.

She was a movie legend, of course, and the instant I lay eyes on her, I understood why. It was more than just her angular face, with features so delicate they reminded me of porcelain. It was more than the designer suit she wore—no, *rocked*—as she walked toward me, looking both elegant and sexy at the same time. It was more than the dark sunglasses that seemed to cover half her face, as if telling the world she knew what they wanted to see, but she wasn't going to give it to them.

No, Marion Hennessey moved with the easy confidence of a woman who knew she was all that. She looked how I felt the previous day as I led Anthony Chekov to Jake's waiting cop car, only without the glob of guacamole on her face. Marion Hennessey looked like she had never had so much as a hair out of place in her life.

She was, in a word, breathtaking.

A couple of people were following after her, failing at being subtle about it, but if she knew about them—and I was sure she did—she didn't show it. A woman to her right ducked into the coffee shop, and Marion walked right up to me and took the seat across from me.

I wasn't the kind of woman who was rendered speechless very often. But this was a new one. What was I supposed to say? "Sorry, I'm waiting for somebody"? Marion Hennessey gave the impression that there was no one in the world more important than her.

"Charlotte Gibson?" Marion asked, reaching a hand out for me to shake. Her voice had a bit of an English affection, but I knew it was fake. Marion Hennessey was born in Lima, Iowa.

"How do you know my name?" I replied. *Cool. I love it when my mouth opens before my brain decides whether it's a good idea.*

To her credit, Marion didn't look taken aback. In fact, she barely reacted at all. The corner of her mouth, painted perfectly in a deep red, twisted upward almost imperceptibly, and she tilted her head a little bit to the right. "Well, you might be the private investigator, but even I'm capable of learning the names of the people I want to hire."

"Your assistant called me," I said, more statement than question as realization dawned upon me. "You're her client, who wants to hire me."

"Indeed," Marion said. Her voice was naturally on the lower end of the register, and she spoke quietly, as if every word she said was a secret between the two of us. I was all too aware of the growing crowd near us. Word must have gotten around, and everyone in the vicinity wanted to catch a glimpse of Marion Hennessey seated with some nobody.

A moment later, the woman who had arrived with Marion returned, a coffee cup in hand. She gave it to Marion, who thanked her, and the woman moved to the side and sat at another nearby empty table while I continued the weirdest conversation of my life.

How do you speak to someone ultra-famous? I mean, sure, I'd met celebrities before. Dave Grohl got coffee from a shop where I was a barista once. Really nice guy, friendly, approachable. But Marion Hennessey was next-level. I kind of got the impression that if I said something wrong in front of her, she could just command a bolt of lightning to fall from the sky and smite me right here in this chair.

Which was ridiculous.

Probably.

Marion took the initiative in the conversation. "Did you hear about the incident at the Maui Diamond Resort yesterday?" she asked, leaning forward in her chair.

"I heard the basics on the radio," I found myself replying. "You were having drinks with others at the restaurant on the beach there, and someone in your party had a medical incident. Is that correct?"

"It is," Marion said. Then her voice went so quiet it was almost inaudible, especially over the sounds of the growing crowd nearby. "This morning I was told that Crystal, my yoga instructor and one of the women I was having drinks with, died."

"Oh, I'm so sorry."

"Thank you. Worse than that, however, is her manner of death. They are obviously waiting for the official toxicology reports to come back, but the initial indication is that Crystal was poisoned. I want to hire you to find the person who poisoned her, because I believe it was meant for me."

I sat in stunned silence for a moment before answering. "No kidding. What makes you think that? Have you told the police?"

"I have. And, while I have all the respect in the world for the Maui Police, and I'm sure they will do an excellent job investigating, I happen to rather enjoy my life, and all things being equal, I'd like to keep living it. Seeing as someone appears intent on killing me, I'm not going to sit around and wait for them to try a second time. That's why I'm hiring you. I want you to do your own investigation, and hopefully between you and the police, the person responsible will be caught before they make another attempt."

"Right. Why do you believe the poison was meant for you?"

"I traded drinks with Crystal at the last second," Marion explained. As the conversation continued, she'd lost the British accent, and sounded more and more American. It was as if she was dropping the façade of the character she had created and sat before me now as she really was: an ordinary woman who was scared for her life.

Well, as ordinary as a woman who owned her own plane could be, anyway.

I looked around at the growing crowd. Two men,

huge, both with bald heads and earpieces, stood nearby, keeping people back from us. They didn't look like mall security, and so I imagined they were Marion's private crew. "Is there somewhere more private we can go to discuss this? If I'm going to be investigating your potential murder, I think it would help to be away from prying ears. Not to mention, I'm sure the Rock and the Rock's brother over there are great, but you're still pretty exposed here right now. I don't want you murdered out here during this conversation, and I certainly don't want to become collateral damage."

Marion pursed her lips ever so slightly. "You're right, of course. A very good point. Come with me."

She stood, and the crowd went nuts. The two bodyguards immediately flanked Marion, and she began walking toward the exit.

"Come on," a voice at my right said. It was the assistant, who took me by the elbow, and I quickly scampered after the group, trying not to be left behind, or trampled by the hordes now following after us. Marion was led to the back seat of an enormous SUV, and I stepped in after her, followed by the assistant. As soon as the door shut behind us, the noise from the crowd disappeared, and Marion seemed to relax a little bit.

"You're right. This is much better," she said. "We'll just drive around for a little bit while we speak."

I pulled out a notebook and pen from my purse. "Right. If I'm going to do this, I need to know everything you can tell me about the drinks you had the other day. Let's start with when you were there, and who you were with."

Marion sat up straighter and removed her sunglasses. Her eyes were a brilliant blue, shimmering with intelligence as she eyed me carefully. "It was a casual thing. There was me, and Amber, of course."

The assistant nodded, the corner of her mouth turning upward in acknowledgement. So that was the assistant's name. I marked it down.

"It was just after my yoga class. Crystal was my instructor; we had private lessons three times a week whenever I was on the island. When we reached the restaurant, she ran into two other instructors that she knew, and we joined them at their table."

"And what were their names?"

"Aaron and Cosmic Pegasus."

I raised an eyebrow skyward. "Cosmic Pegasus? Really?"

Marion shrugged. "What can I tell you? A flower child. Or at least, putting on a persona as such. We were joined soon afterward by Rowan McLeod. He had sent me a text earlier telling me he was on the island and suggested we meet up."

"Oh," I said, trying not to sound super impressed. Rowan McLeod was a Hollywood superstar in his own right.

"That's all. But none of them would have poisoned me. I'm sure of it."

My eyes darted to Amber for only a split second, but she still noticed.

"Don't worry, it wasn't me," she said airily, seemingly not taking the least bit of offense to the fact that I'd just low-key considered her a murder suspect. Amber had brown hair tied back into a ponytail and was dressed casually, an enormous designer purse at her feet that seemed to carry everything Marion could ever need. "Do you know how much Marion pays me? It's a lot. Way more than I would get anywhere else. I've been working for her for seven years, and this isn't a *Devil Wears Prada* situation. I couldn't ask for a better job, and if someone murders Marion, I'm afraid I'll have to find one. I want this killer found as much as you do." She looked over at her employer with a grateful smile.

"Amber is the one who suggested hiring you," Marion explained. "I told her I wanted to hire someone else to work this case for me, separately from the police."

"I heard a podcast about how you were responsible for finding who killed that man from New York a few months ago," Amber chimed in.

"So, Amber didn't do it," I said with a smile, although I mentally didn't cross her off my list just yet. Just because she didn't have an obvious motive didn't mean there wasn't a hidden one I couldn't see yet.

"I didn't."

"Okay, so tell me about these other people. Do you have a last name for Aaron?"

"Lewis. He was at the table with Cosmic Pegasus when we arrived."

"Do you have a last name for Cosmic Pegasus?

Unless Pegasus *is* the last name," I said with a small smile.

Marion shot me a your-guess-is-as-good-as-mine look.

"Aaron runs his own yoga studio," Amber said. "Marion used to see him, before she changed to Crystal due to scheduling conflicts. It's in Wailea; he sees all the super-rich people."

I pulled out my phone and typed "Wailea yoga studio Aaron" into the search bar. The first result was for a studio called "Spiritual Stretch." I clicked it and was immediately greeted by a woman who obviously had had surgery to get a few vertebrae removed, because there was no other explanation as to how she got into that position.

Scrolling past the human slinky on the front page I eventually found a link to an "about us" page. I quickly found a photo of a man doing yoga. Topless, undoubtedly so he could show off his six-pack and full sleeve tattoo. Holding his entire body up on one arm, in a pose I assumed was called "the show-off," his face was turned toward the camera, his gaze seductive. It was as if he was saying "I'll show you a downward dog we can do on this mat that has nothing to do with yoga."

"Is this him?" I asked Marion, turning the phone toward her. She nodded curtly.

"It is."

"Okay. And Cosmic Pegasus?"

"I'm afraid I don't know," Amber said. "She's a yoga instructor as well."

"That's fine. I'm sure there can't be too many

people by that name on the island. I'll find her. And Crystal?"

"Crystal Harris," Marion replied. "She's been my yoga instructor on the island for the last few months. Obviously, she didn't kill me, since she's the one who ended up dead."

"Of course. I'm just gathering background information on everyone who was there. Rowan McLeod?"

"It wasn't Rowan," Marion said shortly. "We worked together on a movie last year, and we got along just fine."

"Okay," I said noncommittally. "I'm still going to have to speak with him, though. He might know something that will help."

"Amber will get you his number."

"Good. Now, can you run me through what happened yesterday? Don't leave anything out."

Marion nodded almost imperceptibly, taking a deep breath before telling her story. "As you may know, I've just wrapped up filming on the sequel to *Divine*, where I play the mother of a famous Broadway actress. You've seen it, yes?"

"Absolutely, I loved you in it," I lied. *Divine* was one of those hoity-toity movies that was nominated for every Oscar under the sun. Marion had won Best Supporting Actress, of course, and it had gotten the award for Best Picture as well, but it was not at all my kind of movie. I wanted jokes, fun scenes, and action rather than people looking forlornly at one another as they forgave each other for past mistakes.

"Great," Marion replied, obviously pleased. "Anyway, when filming wrapped up, I decided I needed a vacation before we begin the promotional tour for the movie. So I've come to the island for a month or so. I see Crystal three times a week, always at three in the afternoon. She comes to my hotel, and we have a private session on the balcony of my suite. Then we go down to the beachside bar for drinks. The staff there know to expect us, so they keep a table for us."

I couldn't begin to imagine how much a one-month stay in a suite at the Maui Diamond Resort with a large enough balcony to have two women doing yoga on it would cost. I could probably buy a small apartment for what Marion Hennessey was spending on a hotel this month.

"Anyway, Crystal and I had our yoga session, as we always do. There was nothing out of the ordinary about it at all. When we were finished, we both showered, changed, and went down to the bar, where Amber was already waiting for us. We were being led to our regular table when Crystal spotted Aaron and Cosmic Pegasus. She said hello, and Aaron invited us to join them, and we did. Amber came over from our regular table."

"Do you think Crystal could have told them ahead of time about your habits?"

Marion's eyes widened slightly; she'd obviously never considered the possibility. "I suppose it's possible. You can't think Crystal had anything to do with this, though. She wouldn't have drunk the pina colada if she had."

I motioned for Marion to continue her story, and

she did. "Anyway, Rowan joined us about fifteen minutes later. We were on our second round of drinks when it all happened. I'd ordered a pina colada, and Crystal got a paloma. When we got our drinks, however, Crystal realized she had just been prescribed a medication for an ear infection that interacts with grapefruit juice. Well, I'm rather a fan of palomas myself, so I suggested we simply switch drinks, as I hadn't touched mine yet. She agreed, and she took my pina colada."

At this point, Marion paused. She pressed her lips together and closed her eyes, her nostrils flaring slightly as she inhaled deeply before continuing. "After a few minutes, Crystal began drinking more quickly. She started complaining that her mouth felt dry. It quickly became apparent that something was very wrong. Crystal kept opening and closing her mouth, and slurring her words. I frankly thought she'd been roofied. Then, out of nowhere, she collapsed. It was horrible. Truly horrible."

"I did a first aid course a while back," Amber chimed in. "So I immediately jumped down and tried to help, while shouting for someone to call 911."

"I did that," Marion said. "I told them to get an ambulance here, and fast. Amber was incredible. She did everything she could until the paramedics arrived. They took Crystal with them."

"What did you think had happened at the time?" I asked.

"I thought she had a heart attack. Of course, Crystal was very young for that to happen. In her mid-thirties, if I had to guess. But sometimes people have undiagnosed issues, don't they?"

"That's what I thought too," Amber agreed. "You just don't expect someone to be poisoned in front of you like that."

"And so Crystal was taken to the hospital. What did you do after that?"

"Well, we followed after her, of course," Marion said. "We waited for around an hour, and then a doctor emerged and gave us the bad news that she'd passed away. Truly horrible. I went back to the hotel, and late last night was visited by the police. They were the ones who said Crystal had been poisoned."

"Okay. When you were at the bar, did you have any food?"

"No. We'd ordered some tapas, but they hadn't arrived yet. We only had our drinks."

"So that means the poison had to be in the pina colada," I muttered.

"There's no other explanation. And no one could have known Crystal and I were going to switch drinks."

It certainly sounded to me like Marion had it right. Someone was trying to kill her.

"I'm warning you, this next part isn't going to be easy," I told her. "Believe me. Knowing someone out there wants you dead sucks a lot. It's hard. I ran away to Hawaii in order to keep my head, and frankly, if you could get off the island for a little while, that might be best. Spend a month in Europe or somewhere by yourself, away from everyone you know."

Marion's lips curled into a small smile. "While you

may have the ability to travel with the advantage of relative anonymity, that is not a luxury that is afforded to me. If someone wants to murder me, I'm not difficult to find. I'm certain there are photos and videos of our conversation outside Honolulu Coffee on the internet as we speak. Besides, I will not allow myself to be cowed by whoever thinks they're going to take my life. I am taking steps to prevent their success by hiring you, and by putting my faith in the Maui Police to get to the bottom of this. But what I will not do is hide myself away. That would be giving my assailant more power than I'm willing to give him. Or her."

A tingle ran down my spine as Marion pronounced those words. She spoke so clearly, and with so much power behind her, that I truly felt as if I was in the presence of more than just another human being.

Marion Hennessey was a freaking *queen.*

"I need Rowan's contact information. I'll need to speak with him."

"That's fine, Amber will send it to you. She'll let his people know I've hired you to look into this."

"Okay. I think that's everything I need for now."

"Good. My driver will drop you off wherever you need." It was then that I realized we were parked in front of the Maui Diamond Resort, and a moment later the door was opened. "Thank you again for the help, Charlie. Now, if you'll excuse me, I rather need to get into the pool. I'm feeling rather dishevelled in this heat."

"If you're dishevelled right now, then I'm a piece of wilted lettuce that's just been stepped on," I replied.

Seriously. The woman looked like she could step right out of the car and onto the red carpet.

Marion laughed, the light sound dancing melodically through the vehicle. "I like you, Charlie. I'll be in touch. All the best."

"Thank you. You too."

Amber shot me a smile and a nod as she followed after her boss, and a moment later the SUV was back on the main road, the driver looking at me through the rear-view mirror.

"Where to, ma'am?"

I was tempted to answer "Wonderland", because there was no way this was actually real.

Chapter 4

I finished my coffee as the chauffeur drove me back to the mall so I could pick up Queenie and go back home, checking my phone for information about Cosmic Pegasus.

She wasn't hard to find, obviously. She ran her own yoga programs but didn't seem to have a website. Instead, Cosmic Pegasus only had a Facebook page. She offered ten different classes a week, and it appeared she specialized in what was my new worst nightmare. Move over, spiders with wings and decaf coffee. The most horrifying thing in the world was now stand-up paddleboard yoga.

I looked at the picture on my screen in a mixture of admiration and horror. Sure, I knew stand-up paddleboarding existed, and I knew yoga existed, but combining the two? No, thank you. Those people already looked like they were way too athletic for me. How on earth they managed to stand on those things and casually glide along the water as if it wasn't the freaking *ocean* was beyond me.

Then you were going to add downward dogs and whatever the names of other yoga poses were to that? No, thank you. That sounded like a recipe for drowning in one of the most embarrassing ways possible.

Either way, Cosmic Pegasus looked exactly how I'd expect someone with a name like that to look. In her business's profile photo, she sat cross-legged on a paddleboard, the sun shining onto her face. The rays kissed her chestnut-brown hair, giving it a reddish hue, and around her forehead was a braided band with a hibiscus flower tucked into it near her temple.

Dressed in a simple tan tank top and a sapphire-blue dress that spilled over the edges of the paddle-board and into the ocean, it gave the impression that Cosmic Pegasus was one with the water as she sat with her eyes closed, hands pressed together at her chest, her lips curled slightly upward in the barest beginnings of a smile.

There was no way I could ever look that peaceful in the ocean.

Anyway, now I knew where I could find her. I was going to have to speak with her. I had a list of people at that table: Aaron, Cosmic Pegasus, Amber, Rowan McLeod. One of them, or possibly a member of the serving staff, was trying to kill Marion Hennessey. I was going to find out who.

The huge SUV slowed down as it turned into the mall parking lot, and I jumped out, thanking the driver. I hopped back into Queenie and headed home.

Vesper, one of my neighbors, was hanging out in her chair by the front door, enjoying a cigarette. "I see you're moving up in the world."

"What do you mean?" I asked.

"Marion Hennessey?"

"How on earth do you know about that already?"

"Honey, that news is already all over the island. I'm pretty sure even TMZ has picked it up."

My mouth dropped open. "You're joking."

"Nope. Everyone wants to know what's going on now that someone at her table died last night. So, tell me, was it murder?"

Vesper leaned forward in her chair, her eyes glimmering with excitement.

I laughed. "If I tell you, do you promise not to call *People* magazine with the info?"

Vesper grinned. "If I've got no other choice. Come on, tell me. I will keep it to myself. I love celebrity gossip, and I desperately want to know what's going on here. Did you know that back in the eighties I dated one of Hollywood's leading men? We only lasted a few weeks. He was here shooting a movie, and I had a small role. After all, when I was a pro surfer, my body was smoking, so I did a few tiny acting gigs on the side. But oh, they were some of the most exciting weeks of my life."

"Okay, now I have to ask: what star was it?" Vesper obviously wanted me to ask the question.

"Now, now. A true lady never tells."

"Vesper, you have a prosthetic leg you use to hit

people and you swear like a sailor. You're a lot of things, but a proper lady is not one of them."

Vesper cackled in amusement, and she took another drag of her cigarette. "You may have a point there, Charlie. All right, I'll just say this: he raided my lost ark over and over and over."

That wasn't a metaphor I needed in my life. Of course, this was Vesper we were talking about. The odds were pretty good that Harrison Ford had simply smiled at her on set and moved on, and that the rest of the story was a figment of her imagination. But now I was curious; I was going to have to ask Leslie about it during my next shift at Aloha Ice Cream.

I perched myself on the stone wall that lined the walkway toward the building's main entrance, crossing my legs at the ankles as I looked at Vesper. "So, what can you tell me about Marion Hennessey?" After all, I had Google, but in my experience, knowing someone who was way too into celebrity gossip was a much better source.

"Oh, I thought you'd never ask. But first, tell me: why did she hire you to investigate?"

"Because her yoga instructor was murdered," I replied. "She wants to make sure the perpetrator is brought to justice."

Vesper gave me a scandalous look. "No! I *thought* so. I even said as much to Leslie this morning, but Leslie doesn't care about that sort of thing."

"So, what can you tell me about Marion?"

"Well, she's a legend, of course. A star who shines bright. Is she as elegant in person as she seems?"

"She is," I confirmed. "I look like a bag of potatoes next to her."

"That makes me so happy to hear," Vesper said dreamily. "And is she as much of a bitch?"

"Excuse me?"

"Marion has this reputation for being a bit of a diva. Not the type who will throw a bowl of M&M's across the room because an assistant forgot to pick out all the green ones, mind you. But the kind of diva who has high standards and expects everyone to live up to them. Apparently, she fired her last agent for not getting her a good enough deal on selling the first photos of her grandchildren."

I raised my eyebrows. "Wow. Well, I didn't get that vibe from her. She was friendly. Easy to talk to. She didn't take offense to anything I said, and we all know I speak before I think a fair bit."

Vespa chuckled lightly. "All the best people do. Anyway, the thing about Marion is that while she's a star, she's quickly becoming a black hole. That's what stars do when they explode, right?"

I shrugged. "I'm sure Zoe would know the answer to that. It sounds good to me. So you're saying she's not as famous as she was?"

"She's still famous, she just hasn't made a splash anywhere except the gossip magazines in the last few years. Her last Oscar nomination was for *Divine*, and that was made in what, 2006? Years and years ago now, and even longer on a Hollywood timeline. Her last two movies have been total flops. Frankly, she should never have agreed to do either of them. She's Marion

Hennessey, for goodness' sake. It's not like she needs to accept every script she gets given out of desperation. And I get it. *Susanna and Julie* was supposed to be a modern-day version of *Thelma and Louise*, but with older characters. But the writing was just awful, and it killed the whole movie."

"That sucks."

"It does, because the premise was great. I love watching women getting revenge on the men who have wronged them. But it just wasn't good. Neither was the release before that one. But hey, she's just finished shooting another film, and this one is directed by Leon Mayer, and it's a sequel to *Divine*, so here's hoping it sends her star soaring once more."

"What did you mean about the gossip magazines?"

"Oh, Marion has been the darling of the paparazzi everywhere, and for all the wrong reasons. About a year ago she was arrested in LA. A DUI. She hired a PR firm, and she managed to get ahead of it, but her mug shot was still leaked and appeared all over the gossip rags. And then there was the thing with her agent. Basically, Marion needs this new movie to do well. She needs a comeback."

"Do you think this movie will do that for her?"

"Absolutely. It should be a monster. There are some enormous names behind it, and it has a great budget and one of the best writers in Hollywood. Give it another year, and all the bad press about Marion will be replaced with her comeback story, how *Flowers for Natalie* will make her star rise once more. Don't get me wrong, Marion is still a legend. She always will be.

She's been a fixture of Hollywood movies since the eighties, she's won six Oscars, has more Golden Globes than I've had surgeries, and represented Prada for decades. The woman oozes class. She just hasn't quite had the success she's used to these past few years."

"I know exactly what you mean. Okay, tell me about Rowan McLeod."

"Now, if you left me alone in a room with that man, the things I would do to him…"

"I believe it, but how about we stick to stuff that's actually happened in real life?" I said quickly. I'd heard more than enough about Vesper's lost ark for one day.

"Prude," Vesper said, shooting me a wink. "But fine. Rowan McLeod, unlike Marion, is a star on the rise. He had a breakout role as the leading man in one of those rom-coms a few years ago, and he's been the hottest thing in Hollywood ever since. He's on the island right now, shooting a movie with Rihanna. Another romantic comedy. I'm sure it will make millions."

"What about scandals? Is he known for shooting more than just movies?"

Vesper snorted. "Are you kidding? He's Canadian."

"Believe it or not, I'm pretty sure even Canada has bad people."

"Well, Rowan's not one of them. The man is a saint. You know what he was in the news for last year, in LA?" I shook my head. "A lady's dog was being stolen on the beach. Rowan ran after the thief, tackled him, got the dog back, and managed to keep the thief under control until the police arrived to arrest him."

"Wow."

"Anyway, if you meet him, slip him my number, will you? Because I'd like him to slip me a little something, if you know what I mean."

"And, that's my cue to end this conversation. Thanks for the info, Vesper."

"Anytime."

I headed into the apartment building and entered my apartment to find Zoe chopping up some vegetables at the kitchen counter. Coco was begging for baby carrots at her feet; they were the only vegetable she really loved.

"Hey," Zoe greeted me when I walked in. "You're just in time for lunch. I'm making ham-and-salami sandwiches."

"Thanks. Need a hand with anything?"

"You could grab the meat and mustard from the fridge. What were you up to this morning?"

"Marion Hennessey hired me to find out who's trying to kill her."

Zoe raised her eyebrows. "But it was her yoga instructor who died last night, wasn't it?"

"Yeah," I called out as I rifled through the fridge, trying to find the ham. "The drink was meant for Marion, though. She was supposed to be the victim."

"No way. That's awful. For everyone involved."

"Yeah. And it means whoever wants her dead is still out there, and now I've got a client."

"Good. You'll be better at finding the perpetrator than the police."

"I appreciate the vote of confidence. Did you see Crystal last night? The yoga instructor who died?"

Zoe nodded. "Yes, I was working when she was brought in. Mark did everything he could to save her, but it was too late. Botulinum toxin works fast."

"That's nerd talk for Botox, right?"

"Sort of. Botulinum toxin is the poison that causes the disease botulism. Essentially, the toxin paralyzes the muscles. Which, if you're using tiny doses and trying to hit some facial muscles, might make you look a little bit younger. Unfortunately, there are other muscles in the body—like the heart—that we don't want to see paralyzed. And botulinum toxin is horrendously toxic. Crystal would only have had to drink a tiny amount before her death warrant was signed."

"There's something cruelly ironic to the idea that someone tried to kill a Hollywood actress with what's essentially Botox," I mused.

"It would be relatively easy to get access to, especially for someone from LA," Zoe said as she grabbed the big knife and cut our sandwiches. She cut them into four little triangles, the way her mom used to do for us as kids, and I was hit with a wave of nostalgia as I took the first bite. It was like I was seven years old again, feet dangling from the firm wooden chairs in Zoe's family home after we'd come back from a morning playing on the beach.

"That's the thing though—only one of my main suspects is from LA. Rowan McLeod."

"Wow, you're running with the rich and famous now, aren't you?" Zoe asked with a wink.

"They must be famous if even you've heard of them," I teased. Zoe had always been the type to prefer books as a form of entertainment over TV and movies. And she had never been the type to keep up with celebrity gossip, whereas I had read Perez Hilton's blog every single day as a teenager.

"True," Zoe admitted. "This could be a big case for you. It's going to be high-profile."

"You're telling me. We were basically surrounded by fans and people with cameras today. A part of me is scared to check the news right now. There's probably going to be pictures of me drinking my iced coffee and looking like a surprised giraffe when Marion Hennessey sat in front of *me*."

Zoe laughed. "Hey, that's a good thing. You might be a surprised giraffe, but a surprised giraffe who solves the murder is going to get more clients."

"Here's hoping," I said, crossing my fingers as I headed to my room to call Rowan McLeod.

Chapter 5

Rowan answered the phone himself, which took me off guard a little bit.

"Hello?" his sultry voice answered, and my eyes widened as I realized this was it. I was really talking to *the* Rowan McLeod.

"Hi, this is Charlie Gibson," I introduced myself. "I'm working for Marion Hennessey, and she gave me your number. I'm investigating the murder of her yoga instructor Crystal, and I'm wondering if the two of us could have a chat sometime, just so you can tell me what you remember about that night."

"Sure thing," Rowan replied. "I'm filming most of the day, but I should be back at the hotel around seven. If you'd like, I can meet you at the bar afterward."

"Great."

We worked out the details, and I hung up the phone then headed back into the living room to tell Zoe my news.

"Don't tell Vesper about my date. She'll be jealous," I said when I let Zoe know where I'd be that night.

Zoe laughed. "I thought Vesper was happily single."

"Single doesn't mean celibate. Apparently she has a thing for Hollywood stars. Ask her about the weeks she spent with Harrison Ford that I'm about eighty percent sure is totally made up."

Before Zoe got the chance to reply, my phone pinged, indicating that I'd gotten a text. I glanced at the screen to see it was from Dot.

Looks like someone is famous. Please tell me we have another murder to investigate. Florence Ulrich wants me to go to the hairdresser with her so she can tell me about this new hemorrhoid cream she's got, and if I have to listen to that for an hour I'm afraid we might end up with another dead body on the island.

A second later another text came through, this one a link to *TMZ*. I tapped on it and found myself staring at a picture of Marion and myself at Honolulu Coffee.

Marion, of course, was stunning. She looked like a statue, her eyes hidden behind her sunglasses as she leaned elegantly toward me, one leg hooked over her knee, showing off the red bottoms of her Louboutin heels.

I, on the other hand, had my coffee halfway to my mouth, and had started pursing my lips to take a sip, making me look like I was waiting for Marion to give me the world's most awkward kiss. Cool. This was definitely the photo of me that I wanted thousands of people to see today. Very cool.

"Well, my life is over," I announced to Zoe.

"I'm glad you've given me the heads-up that I have to take over the lease. What's happened this time? Is the grocery store out of your favorite flavor of Doritos?"

"No, this is much worse," I said, handing her my phone.

Zoe took it, and her eyebrows rose. "I told you you'd be famous."

"I kind of figured this might show up on some local news sites and a few people's Instagram stories. This is *TMZ*, Zoe. This is *big*. And of course they had to choose that picture."

"It's cute," Zoe replied with a smile.

"It's not cute. I look like a jellyfish trying to inhale my coffee and Marion at the same time."

"You do not. You're being overly critical. Anyway, the photo is the least important part of this. What does it say?"

"I don't know. I got caught up at the idea of thousands of people clicking on this article and seeing me looking like that, and decided I'm going to be a hermit forever now."

"Well, at least you're not overreacting." Zoe scrolled down past the photo and began to read in her news announcer's voice. "*Marion Hennessey appears to be taking matters into her own hands with regards to the death of her yoga instructor, Crystal Harris. Only hours after the Maui Police announced that the woman's death is being considered a homicide —Hennessey and Rowan McLeod were at the table with Harris when she collapsed—the silver screen star was seen meeting with a woman identified as Charlotte Gibson, a private investigator working on Maui, and who has been responsible for helping solve two murders on Maui in the past year. We reached out to Hennessey's staff and confirmed that Gibson has been hired to find Harris's killer.*"

"Hey, the photo aside, at least this is good publicity for me, right?"

"Totally," Zoe replied with a grin. "This is a good thing."

"And now, the pressure is on. I have to crack this case."

I took my phone back from Zoe and typed a reply to Dot. *Tell Florence you need to cancel. You have a murder to help me solve.*

Her reply came through a moment later. *Thank goodness. I was going to have to make up a good lie, otherwise. And Florence always knows when I'm lying. Let me know what you need.*

Thanks. I will. I'm not one hundred percent sure yet. Maybe nab some security footage from the Maui Diamond Resort bar, and the lobby, just in case?

On it. I'll text you when I've got something.

"Wow, this is all over the gossip sites," Zoe said a moment later. "And there are other photos. So don't worry, not everyone is going to see the picture you hate."

"That's something, at least. I didn't think of that. I mean, sure, I knew there was a crowd around Marion. But I never imagined I'd find myself on the *TMZ* website. That's insane. I don't think I'm actually processing it completely. It feels like it's something happening to somebody else. Anyway, I have a meeting with Rowan McLeod later tonight, but I'd like to stop by Aaron's yoga studio and have a chat with him."

"Sounds good. I'm heading to the hospital in about an hour. I'm working a double shift, so you're going to have to make your own dinner. Do I have to remind you to eat a vegetable occasionally?" Zoe asked with a grin.

"Please. I have Doritos in the cupboard, and they're made with corn, so that counts."

"If your organs could talk, I bet they would beg me to put them out of their misery."

"I also bought passionfruit cream cheese at the farmer's market this morning."

"I suppose that's better," Zoe replied, looking unimpressed.

"Sorry we haven't all been to medical school."

"You don't need to be a doctor to figure out Doritos aren't a food group."

"They're not a food group by themselves, but they count as a vegetable."

"They absolutely do not."

"Close enough. Anyway, I'll see you later. Have fun at work. Try not to have to extract too many things from people's butts."

If I'd learned anything from Zoe's work stories, it was that people would stick anything up there.

"I'll try," she said with a laugh. "Good luck with your investigation."

ACCORDING TO HIS WEBSITE, AARON'S YOGA STUDIO, Spiritual Stretch, was located in Wailea. Situated above the golf course, the studio was in a single-level, cream-colored building surrounded by lush greenery. Asian-inspired decoration abounded, with a wooden arched pergola on which a golden pothos plant climbed. I crossed beneath the plant and over a small bamboo bridge that spanned a miniature stream, two seated Buddha statues guarding the front of it.

I reached a large, double wooden door with a circular pattern carved into it and passed through. Inside, fragrant incense reached my nostrils as the soft notes of a bamboo flute floated across the space. Soft lighting filled the space, where behind a wooden desk sat a woman in her twenties. Her black hair was tied in a loose bun at the nape of her neck, and she wore a plain, charcoal-gray scoop-neck T-shirt.

"Hello," she greeted me in a soft voice. "Welcome to Spiritual Stretch. Are you here for our twelve o'clock session?"

"Um, no. I was hoping to speak with Aaron. I'm here on behalf of Marion Hennessey, and I'm investigating the death of Crystal Harris at the Maui Diamond Resort the other night. Marion told me Aaron was one of the people at the table that night."

The woman's eyes widened. "Oh. Of course. Let me just see. Have a seat over there, and I'll find Aaron for you."

I glanced at my phone screen to check the time as she scurried off. It was just after eleven thirty. Luckily, that meant I had half an hour before the next session started. My eyes scanned the space, looking for a chair, but the only available seating appeared to be earth-tone linen cushions on the floor. I had seen Aaron Lewis doing yoga on his web page. The last thing I wanted was for him to see me struggle to get up off those cushions if I sat down. So, I stood in place until the receptionist returned a moment later, followed by the man in question.

I recognized him from his website and briefly wondered if the man had ever heard of T-shirts. All he wore was a pair of sage-gray yoga pants, which rested so low on his hips I was terrified at how close the man was to a wardrobe malfunction.

"Aaron Lewis, owner of Spiritual Stretch," he said to me, holding out a hand, which I shook. "Come with me. We can speak out on the balcony, where we'll have some privacy."

I followed Aaron past a latticed wall and through to the studio, whose view took my breath away. It looked like any standard yoga studio, but with floor-to-ceiling French doors that looked out over the golf course and to the Pacific Ocean beyond. Aaron opened the doors, which led onto a large wooden deck stained weathered gray. He walked to the edge and crouched down, placing his hands on the deck before dropping his legs over the ledge and letting them dangle.

"Uh, yeah, I'm not going to try doing it that way," I said as I awkwardly sat myself down on the ledge about three feet from him.

Aaron laughed. "We can't all be as fit as I am."

Well, at least he was humble.

"So," Aaron continued. "Marion has hired you to find the killer, has she?"

"Yes. She was very fond of Crystal and wants to do everything in her power to ensure her killer is brought to justice." I figured sticking with the official story was the way to go. After all, somebody out there wanted Marion Hennessey dead, and I didn't want to tip them off that I was onto them. "Can you tell me how you ended up at the bar last night?"

"I was there with Cosmic Pegasus. The two of us are casually seeing each other, though it's not serious. I'm very available. I'm very skilled, and it would be a crime to only allow one woman to experience the pleasure I can give them."

I involuntarily began to gag, covering it up with a cough.

"Anyway," he continued, "the two of us arrived a little after three. Cos had the night off, and I didn't have a session until seven o'clock, so I figured we could have drinks, and then there'd be a bit of time for me to get some before my session."

Aaron glanced over at me and gave me what he probably thought were bedroom eyes but screamed, "I'm going to hide your body in my basement freezer under chicken drumsticks" instead.

I rolled my eyes. "So you got to the bar a little after three. Then what?"

"Well, Cos and I chatted for a bit. Then, Crystal and Marion walked past, and Crystal stopped to say hi. I invited them to sit with us, and Marion agreed. She called Amber over, who joined us straight away. Then

Rowan McLeod was walking along the beach; he spotted Marion and came over himself. That's everyone who was at the table. The waitress came by and gave us our drinks, and the next thing I knew Crystal was lying on the ground having some sort of seizure."

"Did you notice anyone near the drinks?"

"We all were," Aaron said with a shrug. "When they arrived, the waitress put them all on the table, and it was a flurry of arms and hands as we all grabbed ours. If you're asking whether I saw someone slip poison into Crystal's drink, the answer is no. But then, I was focused on my own. Gin and tonic. I don't like overly sweet drinks, or heavy ones. I like to keep my body feeling lithe and nimble at all times."

I quickly asked my next question before Aaron had a chance to tell me just how nimble he could be. "Did you know Marion before this?"

"Yes. In fact, she used to be a client of mine, before Crystal got her claws into her. I suppose I shouldn't say that about the dead, but it's true."

I raised an eyebrow. "I didn't realize the yoga industry was so vicious."

"I'm not in this business because I love asanas more than anything. I love money, and I'm in this because it's the best way I know how to make it. I take rich, older women whose husbands won't touch them anymore and show them a man who can do a scorpion handstand *and* still makes them feel like they're desirable as the perky twenty-something secretary at his office, even if they can barely do a downward dog. They're willing to dump truckloads of money into my business to feel young and sexy again, and if that means I have to touch a wrinkly old ass from time to time, well, so be it."

Every time I thought this was the peak, surely Aaron couldn't be a worse human being, he always seemed to be able to prove me wrong.

"So you were mad at Crystal for stealing your client?" I asked pointedly.

Aaron nodded, frowning as he did so, and then realized what that meant. "Yes. I mean, okay, I was kind of mad. But not enough to kill her!"

"Are you sure? Being able to advertise to all those women that one of the most famous movie stars in the world is also your client had to bring you in some business."

"Please. I didn't need her. My abs do all the talking for me."

I kind of wished his abs would start talking now, so I wouldn't have to listen to the words coming out of his mouth.

"So you were mad, but not enough to kill her? Help me out here, Aaron."

"Fine. I was upset. Marion pays well, and she tips. But I got over it."

"Why did Marion leave you for Crystal?"

"Crystal only sees—saw—private clients. She didn't run a studio like I do. That meant she had a more flexible schedule, which suited Marion better. Was it a blow to my ego? Yes. Would I have preferred for Marion to work her schedule around me so that I could continue seeing her? Yes. But that's not how it went, and that's okay. I got over it, and I certainly didn't kill Crystal. Besides, all this happened months ago. If I wanted to kill her, it would have been when this all went down. I've moved on."

I quickly realized the problem with hiding my true motive here as a detective: I couldn't straight-up ask Aaron about his relationship with Marion and whether he'd have any reason to kill *her*. Luckily, he didn't seem to be the sharpest knife in the drawer, and despite his bravado, I was willing to bet his ego had the tensile strength of a piece of glass.

"I don't believe you. A woman like Marion, rejecting you? I bet you weren't angry with Crystal; you were angry with Marion. After all, look at your body. She should have been the one making changes in her schedule to be with you, not the other way around. I bet that's how you saw it. She was an ungrateful cow who didn't appreciate what she had with you."

"Damn straight," Aaron snapped. "I bet she's a lesbian or something."

"Right, because the only reason a woman wouldn't want to be around you is if she's only attracted to other women."

"Exactly. Do you know how much work I put into this body? I lead four yoga sessions a day, five days a week, and I have private clients on the side. I've made a fortune running one of the most successful yoga studios in the state of Hawaii, and she thinks she can just up and leave me for some hippie who thinks shiny rocks prevent the flu and that her relationships are affected when Mercury is in retrograde? Idiot. Total idiot."

"I know I'm going to regret asking this, but were you and Marion... you know... doing it?"

"No. She never would have fired me and gone with Crystal as her instructor if we had. She would have known what she would be missing. Our relationship was always professional, but nonetheless, I was a better professional than Crystal. And while I don't begrudge her, yeah, I'm mad that Marion is no longer my client. Do you know how easy it is to convince older women to come to my classes when I can tell them that *Marion Hennessey* of all people uses me as her instructor? It's like taking candy from a baby, only the candy is sweet, sweet hundred dollar bills."

"Right. I'd be mad, too, if I were you."

"Whatever. I don't need that bitch anyway. Sorry. I know she's hired you to find Crystal's killer, and I hope you succeed, but I am bitter about her leaving me. I put so much effort into my business, and she goes ahead and ruins one of the best things I have going."

"Were you polite to her at the bar the other night, at least?"

"Obviously. I'm not an idiot. She might have fired me as an instructor, but she's one of the most famous women in the world. I'm not going to burn that bridge, and if you repeat anything that I'm telling you now, I'll deny it. I can be very persuasive."

Not persuasive enough to keep Marion as a client, I thought to myself, but I wisely managed to keep my mouth shut. After all, I didn't want to alienate Aaron while he was making himself out to be such a good suspect for this murder.

"What about the others?" I asked. "Was anyone being particularly rude to Crystal, or Marion, or anyone else?"

"No. It was a very pleasant time, and we were all enjoying ourselves until Crystal... well..." Aaron trailed off. "The conversation was very light. Have you spoken to the staff working at the resort yet?"

"I haven't had the chance. Why? Do you think one of them might have done it?"

"I imagine it would have to be. Who else would kill Crystal? Rowan McLeod didn't know her at all, as far as I could tell. Cos didn't have anything against her, and I certainly didn't do it. And if Marion was upset with Crystal, the two of them wouldn't have gone drinking together, would they? That assistant of Marion's seemed totally happy, too. No, it doesn't make any sense for it to have been any of us. I bet it was one of the staff. I'd speak with them."

"Okay, thanks. Hey, just one more thing: do you have access to Botox here?"

Aaron shrugged. "I don't use it. I prefer to keep my skin looking great the old-fashioned way: exercise, a vegan diet, and natural skincare products. I'm sure if you're interested, some of my clients could procure some for you, though. Would you like me to look into that for you?"

"I'm good. I was just curious. I think that's all I need for now."

"Happy to help. Hopefully you find the killer. And listen, I've still got twenty minutes until my next session, if you wanted to get a quick workout in with me," Aaron said, shooting me a wink.

"Okay, let me make one thing clear: I would rather set myself on fire than have sex with you, so if we can stick to the facts from that night from now on instead of you telling me how you use your dick as a divining rod, that would be great."

"You don't even know me. I'm a yoga master. I can bend and flex in ways you can't even imagine."

"And you're going to have to imagine all the things I could do, because I am leaving."

I got up from the deck.

"Aw, come on. Are you sure? No strings attached. I promise you nothing but a good time."

"I have never been more sure of anything in my life. I'll be in touch if I need anything else."

"Lesbian," I heard Aaron mutter under his breath as I left.

That was fine with me. As far as I was concerned, he could nama-stay the hell away from me.

I headed back into the studio and retraced my steps to return to the reception area and go home to shower in bleach. Aaron Lewis was creepy as anything, and had admitted he was angry with Marion for having fired him as her yoga instructor.

He was easily at the top of my suspect list right now.

Chapter 6

Since I still had a few hours to kill before meeting Rowan, and Zoe would be at the hospital, I dialed Dot and put her on speaker as I drove back up the road toward Kihei.

"Mind if I come over for a bit? We can run over the basics on this case."

"Sure. I'll give Rosie a call as well. She'll be upset if she doesn't get to involve herself in this."

"There's no one in the world I'm more terrified of than Rosie."

"I like to believe *I'm* the most terrifying person you know," Dot replied.

"You're a close second."

"I suppose I can live with that."

"You're going to have to, because I've never seen you snap a person's neck as easily as if it was a chicken wing."

"Just because you've never seen it happen doesn't mean I haven't done it."

"Sure. I totally believe you, Dot. Anyway, I'll see you in about ten minutes. I've already got a suspect I hope did it."

Dot chuckled on the end of the line. "And you're only a few hours into your investigation? He must be a piece of work."

"You have no idea. I'd love nothing more than to watch Jake slap the cuffs on him."

"Speaking of your favorite neighbor, I saw him on the news earlier. He and Liam are running the investigation into Crystal's death."

"Oh, great. Well, if I'm subtle enough, neither one of them will ever have to know that I'm also investigating. Not until I hand them Aaron's head on a platter, anyway."

"Seeing as your face is plastered all over every entertainment website on the internet, I think they're going to figure it out pretty quickly. Anyway, I'll see you soon."

Dot disconnected the call, and I focused entirely on the road. I stopped by Maui Pie on the way and picked up a lilikoi cream pie. I figured it might help me forget the heebie-jeebies I got from Aaron.

Pie always made everything better.

I beat Rosie to Dot's apartment by about two minutes, and I was just in the kitchen cutting up the pie and trying to get the slices onto plates without causing too much of a disaster when Rosie knocked at the door.

"I'll get it," Dot said, jumping up from her chair at

the computer. She opened the door, and Rosie entered. The two of them immediately made their way to the kitchen to get a slice of pie.

"I hear you've got yourself a new case," Rosie said with a smile. "At least three people have texted me asking if the young woman spotted drinking coffee with Marion Hennessey is the same one I'm friends with."

"I do. And it's actually bigger than solving a murder. Marion's life is on the line." I recounted the entire story to Rosie, who listened intently.

When I was finished, she pursed her lips. "Yes. It appears in this situation, the stakes are quite high. What have you got so far, Dot?"

"Well, I've managed to find the security camera footage from the bar in question. Unfortunately, they don't have any angles of the table where the group was seated. It would have been all too easy to solve this case if we had video footage of the poisoning in question. *But*, I still found something interesting."

Dot took a big bite of pie and then carried her plate over to the computer desk, where she began tapping away while Rosie and I stood behind her, looking at the dual-monitor setup. A video playback screen opened, and Dot fast-forwarded it to a certain timestamp.

"There," she said triumphantly.

It was a shot of about half the bar, with patrons perched on glossy stools ordering from a bartender with shaggy blond hair and an easy smile.

"What are we looking at?" Rosie asked, squinting at the screen.

"Recognize anyone?"

"That guy," I said, pointing to a man at the bottom of the screen. He looked to be in his fifties, with graying hair around his temples. He had a traditionally handsome face, with a chiseled jaw and mischievous eyes, and something about him was familiar. "I know his face, but I don't know from where."

"Likely on screen when watching the Oscars," Dot replied. "That's Bill Jamieson, Marion Hennessey's ex-husband."

"Jamieson and Hennessey, hey?" I said with a small grin. "I can see why they were made for each other."

"Well, unfortunately, the buzz of their marriage eventually turned into a hangover," Dot explained. "Marion and Bill separated after eleven years of marriage, about ten years ago."

"And on the list of people who want Marion Hennessey dead, I have to assume her ex-husband is near the top."

"Exactly," Dot said.

"It was a messy divorce, if I remember correctly, and I do," Rosie said. "Their daughter was grown, so there was no custody dispute, but both parties used the media to full effect to disparage the other. There were rumors that Marion had cheated on Bill. Claims that Bill had secret bank accounts overseas meant to hide money from his wife."

I raised an eyebrow. "I have to admit, I didn't think this was the sort of thing you were interested in."

"Are you kidding? I defected to America for a reason, and Hollywood was a big part of it. Sure, things have changed. It's no longer as much of an *event* when a movie is released as it was when Jayne Mansfield or Marlon Brando were around, but I still keep up with the gossip from Los Angeles," she said with a sly smile.

"Yeah, Rosie is way better at that stuff than me," Dot agreed. "I know the basics, but she can tell you who was in any movie, and she can name all six of Elizabeth Taylor's husbands."

"Seven," Rosie corrected. "Eight if you count Richard Burton twice."

"There you go."

"Okay," I said. "So, Bill Jamieson was at the bar that afternoon, too. And yet, he didn't notice his ex-wife at all? I suppose it's technically *possible*, since it looks like the bar was busy, and they were seated at a table near the beach. But it's unlikely. He definitely didn't say hi. Neither Marion nor Amber mentioned him. They must not have realized he was there."

Rosie turned back to the screen. "Can we see what his hands are doing? Do we see him poisoning the drinks?"

Dot shook her head. "Unfortunately, no. His hands are just out of view from this angle. There's a bit of a blind spot on the bar, and it's exactly there."

I groaned. "Of course, it couldn't have been that easy."

"However, he certainly had the opportunity." Dot tapped away at the screen, and the video footage began to fast-forward. She paused it a moment later. "Here."

Dot had paused the screen on a shot of a waitress

carrying a tray of drinks. Bill had stopped her and asked a question, and she placed the tray of drinks on the bar, just out of the view of the camera.

"Oh, come *on*," I muttered, frustration in me rising. We were literally inches away from being able to see if Bill Jamieson was the man trying to kill Marion, but the drinks being just out of frame meant I couldn't tell for sure.

"We might not be able to see whether or not he's poisoning those drinks, but he certainly had the opportunity," Rosie said. "And the fact that he appears to have created that opportunity himself by stopping a random waitress instead of asking his question to the bartender certainly doesn't make him look less guilty."

"I agree," Dot said.

"I need to talk to Bill. He has to go to the top of the suspect list after seeing this," I said. "Which is too bad. I'm really hoping Aaron Lewis did it. I don't like him at all, but unfortunately someone giving me the heebie-jeebies isn't reason enough to throw them in jail."

"Why would he kill her now, though?" Rosie mused. "They've been divorced for over a decade."

"You don't get it, because you've never had a nasty divorce," Dot said. "It's all about opportunity. If I was driving down the street late at night, no one around, and I spotted Joe on the sidewalk, I might have 'accidentally' swerved and hit the bastard head-on. He took years of my life. It's only fair that I should have gotten to take his. I never got the chance, of course. His heart took care of it for me. And I wouldn't have gone out of my way to kill him. But given the opportunity, if I knew

I could get away with it? I certainly would have considered it."

"Okay, well, homicidal fantasies aside, even if that's all true, it's not actually the case here," I pointed out. "After all, Crystal was poisoned with Botox. I don't know about Bill, but that's not the sort of thing I just carry around with me on a day-to-day basis on the odd chance that I get to murder my ex. And a crowded bar at one of the most popular hotels on Maui isn't exactly a low-stakes situation. He could have been caught at any time. Heck, if that camera had been nudged a few inches in one direction, he would have."

"That's a good point," Dot conceded.

"Nonetheless, he should still remain at the top of the suspect list," Rosie said.

"Oh, he is. I don't like how he just *happened* to stop the waitress carrying the drinks to his ex-wife's table."

"Neither do I," Rosie said.

"And I've got another suspect for you as well," Dot said.

"Wow. And here I was thinking I'd be hard-pressed to find someone who wanted to kill Marion."

"I can't say for sure Amber would have murdered her, but she wasn't as enthusiastic about her job as she made out to be."

"Amber? As in, Marion's personal assistant Amber?"

"That's the one. She has a private Instagram account. No followers, doesn't follow anyone. It took me a little bit of digging to find it; I had to match the

IP addresses the account was accessed from, but it's definitely her."

The mouse flittered across the screen, and a moment later an Instagram feed appeared. There were about a dozen posts, each a blurry photo of nothing particularly identifiable.

"Here's the caption of the latest post," Dot said, clearing her throat a couple of times before changing her voice to that of a dramatic storyteller. "*Today, M was in a mood. I think she read that article in* People *magazine last week that called her washed up. She pretended she didn't, but there was a copy of it in her trash. And I get that it's hard to hear those things, but she takes it out on me and I am sick of it. First, there was the coffee. It wasn't cold enough. Excuse me, bitch, but it's an iced coffee. It's half ice. It's not getting colder. What do you want me to do? Change the laws of physics? If I could do that I certainly wouldn't be working as her assistant. So of course, I go back to the coffee shop, pretend to talk to the barista, bring M her coffee back, and this time it's perfect, and why couldn't I just do it right the first time? World's biggest eye roll. Celebrities, I swear. Some days, I just want to strangle her.*"

I raised my eyebrows as Dot read out that last sentence. "Wow. That's definitely Amber?"

"Without question."

"She made out that her job was great and she loved it. Okay, I'll talk to her. Alone this time, away from Marion. Please tell me you haven't found a reason for Cosmic Pegasus to hate her too."

Dot chuckled. "Not yet, anyway."

"Good. Who knew so many people in the world wanted Marion Hennessey dead?"

"What was she like?" Rosie asked me. "Marion, I mean. Was she as unapproachable and aloof as she makes herself out to be?"

I paused for a moment, pursing my lips slightly as I considered the question. "She certainly wasn't the warmest person I've ever met, but the more we talked, the more relaxed she became. I think it's partly an act, to keep up appearances, but I wouldn't be surprised if she also does it to protect herself. It was certainly something, sitting in that mall and finding myself surrounded by fans and paparazzi. I can't imagine living like that every single day, and I don't blame her for putting walls up."

"She was such a big star in the eighties and nineties," Rosie said wistfully. "But she's made some crummy choices when it comes to her career the last decade or so, and her star doesn't shine as bright as it once did. Still, the movie she's just finished promises to be a good one. She needs a big comeback, and this might be it."

"Here's hoping we don't have a James Dean situation," I muttered. After all, the man's last movie had been released posthumously after his death in a car crash back in the fifties.

"I have faith in you," Dot said, turning to me and shooting me a wink. "You'll solve the case."

"I hope so. On the bright side, Marion knows someone is after her now, so she'll take steps to protect herself more than she ordinarily would."

"Have we considered the serving staff at the bar as suspects?" Rosie asked. "After all, you never know."

"I'm going back to the bar tonight. I was going to ask around then," I replied. "I think it's unlikely, but unlikely doesn't mean impossible."

"Agreed," Rosie said. "There are some crazy people out there. Although I wouldn't expect someone working at the bar at the Maui Diamond to randomly carry around botulism toxin, either."

"No, but Marion often went down there with Crystal after their yoga sessions," I explained. "Any employee who would have wanted her dead would have expected her there. That said, I still find it unlikely, and given as we've got some other great suspects, right now I'm going to focus on them."

"That's a good idea," Dot agreed. "Let us know if you need anything else. Like maybe a bit of company while you speak with Rowan."

I laughed. "Don't tell me you're looking for a sugar daddy."

"Honey, the man is young, he's rich, and he's as good looking as Rock Hudson while actually being straight. You can't blame me for wanting to shoot my shot."

"Okay, well, feel free to shoot it far, far away from me."

"Prude."

"I'll tell you how the dinner goes, though. After all, don't forget he's still a suspect too."

"I know. I'd love to interrogate him. I could make him squeal," Dot said with a grin.

"I don't know about squealing, but this conversation is making me squirm."

"I thought your generation was supposed to be liberated and open about this sort of thing."

"Yeah but not when…" I paused, and Dot's eyes narrowed.

"Not when what?"

Dot wouldn't have taken too kindly to it if I mentioned that she was getting on in years. After all, she famously never admitted to being old.

"Not when it's a friend of mine."

"Yeah, that better be what you thought," Dot said, waving a finger in my face.

"Nice save, kid," Rosie mumbled with a small smile.

"All right," I said with a chuckle. "Enjoy the pie."

"Oh, I already have," Dot said. "Let us know what you find out from Rowan, will you?"

"Will do."

I headed to the door, said goodbye to my friends, and drove home to get ready for my meeting that night.

Chapter 7

As much as I tried to hide it, I was nervous. I tried telling myself that this was like meeting with any other witness to a crime. There was nothing special about Rowan McLeod; he was just another guy who happened to be sitting at the table where a woman died. He was just another murder suspect.

But of course, none of that was true. I could lie to myself as much as I wanted, but Rowan was one of the hottest, richest, and most famous men on the planet. And I wasn't about to show up to a meeting with him looking like Oscar the Grouch.

I wished Zoe was home. She always looked like she was effortlessly put together. She would know what to wear. And how to do my hair. Zoe's bathroom had about eight thousand different hair products on the counter, and I didn't know what any of them did.

After my fifth outfit change—jeans were too casual to meet Rowan McLeod, right?—I threw my clothes on the bed, sighed, and plonked myself down on the edge of it with a huff.

I pulled out my phone and texted Zoe. *Emergency! What do I wear tonight?*

I stared at the screen, anxiously awaiting a reply. I didn't care that Zoe was probably reattaching someone's limb after a car accident. This was an equally important emergency.

About three minutes later, my phone pinged. I dove for it, reading Zoe's reply.

Wear your dark blue skinny jeans. The ones that make your butt look good. And pair it with that black top with the keyhole neckline and long sleeves. Throw on a long gold chain to go with it. And wear heels.

I don't like heels.

Nobody likes heels.

You're the best, Zoe. I love you.

I love you too. Good luck with the meeting. Have fun. I think it's the first time you've asked for fashion advice when talking to a potential murderer.

What can I say? I like making a good first impression.

Zoe replied with a bunch of laughing emojis, and I grinned as I hunted through my now-giant pile of discarded clothes to find the pieces in question. A moment later, my phone pinged again.

For your hair, do a half updo. It's super easy to do with fine hair and looks really classy.

What would I ever do without you? I replied, adding heart emojis to the end of the message. Seriously, Zoe was a lifesaver.

I put on the outfit Zoe suggested, moved to the

bathroom, and did my hair and a bit of makeup, and when I was finished I decided that I probably looked presentable enough to have a drink with a famous Hollywood star.

If this meeting ended up on TMZ, I wasn't going to look like a beached walrus.

Half walking, half stumbling down the stairs—it had been a long time since I'd had to wear heels, okay? —I eventually made it into Queenie's driver's seat without breaking an ankle, and I drove down to the Maui Diamond Resort, in the heart of Wailea's luxury resorts.

I was about ten minutes early, so I seated myself at the bar and ordered a drink as I waited for Rowan. The Beachside Bar and Restaurant was one of the larger venues located in the resort. Inside, a long, sleek black bar housed people looking to drink, while tables and chairs were spread comfortably through the interior and spilled out onto the patio, with the tables furthest out offering beautiful views of the water. The tiki torches that dotted the edge of the patio were lit at night.

I sipped my Coke while I waited.

Being the first to arrive had the added advantage that Rowan wasn't going to see me walking in my heels. Not that I cared what he thought. He was probably just like Marion: a little aloof, a little bit arrogant, knowing that I was just hired help rather than someone he would actually care to know. He was nothing more than just another murder suspect.

"Hi, you must be Charlie," a familiar voice behind

me said suddenly. I turned, smiling, to find myself looking directly at Rowan McLeod, in the flesh. He looked exactly the way he did on screen: amber eyes that shone with excitement. Two days' worth of stubble around a chiseled chin, and a warm, genuine smile that spread across his face and reached his eyes, which creased slightly in the corners.

"Rowan. It's nice to meet you," I said, holding out a hand for him to shake, which he did.

Behind him, an extended family of eight seated at one of the tables gaped openly. I forced myself to look back at him.

"Listen, why don't we grab a booth? It might offer us a bit more privacy," Rowan suggested.

"Sure." After all, every eye in this place was already on Rowan. A couple women in their twenties were openly glowering at me, as if I had single-handedly destroyed their lives. Was this what celebrities lived with every single day?

I slipped off the stool and tried to look confident and sexy as I teetered on my heels toward a table. Not that I cared what he thought, of course. He was a murder suspect, damn it. I kept having to remind myself of that. A man in his thirties came up to us and asked to take a quick selfie with Rowan, and he obliged.

"Thanks, dude," the guy said to Rowan with a grin before rushing back off to his own table.

I felt like a zoo animal as we walked along. Most of the patrons in the bar seemed too scared to approach Rowan and ask for a picture or an autograph, and one of the servers began to scowl at anyone who looked like they were going to try, deterring anyone else from even trying. Obviously, this wasn't her first encounter with a celebrity while she was on shift.

The two of us took a booth at the back of the bar, where we found ourselves in relative privacy. The high-backed seating was leather, with a live-edge wooden table between us. The soft glow from warm industrial-style lighting above us lent the whole place a cozy atmosphere as the server handed each of us a drink menu. She tried to be professional about it, but even I noticed her hand shaking slightly as she handed Rowan his.

"I'll make sure security knows you're here and ensures your privacy," she said when she made sure we were settled.

"Thank you," Rowan said. "We would appreciate that."

When the server left, Rowan began perusing the offerings. "I've got to say, I'm famished. Want to have dinner? I'm buying. The burgers here are out of this world."

Seriously? I was now having dinner with one of the most famous men in Hollywood?

"Sounds good," I replied, trying to sound casual, but I was pretty sure my voice had actually gone about an octave higher than usual. I grabbed the full menu and had a look at the offerings, my mouth watering. That was when I realized all I'd had to eat so far today was a sandwich and a slice of pie. I could definitely go for some food.

My stomach began to grumble as I looked at the pasta on offer.

"Have you eaten here before?" Rowan asked.

I nodded. "Sure have. Although my last meal here didn't end too well."

He grinned at me, and my insides melted. "Bad date?"

"You could say that. I accused her of murder, and she kidnapped me. But luckily, she didn't manage to finish me off."

Rowan's eyes widened with genuine surprise. "Okay, that's not where I thought that story was going. I'll just write that down here: don't… kidnap… Charlie."

I laughed. Rowan was easy to get along with, and I had to remind myself that he was a potential murderer, and I couldn't let myself just get caught up in his charm.

"I shouldn't joke about that, though. Not when Crystal died here just the other day. Which, of course, is why you've come here to speak with me. Marion told me she hired you to find Crystal's killer."

"Yes. I'm hoping you can help me with my investigation."

"Of course, whatever I can do to help. Unfortunately, I don't think I have much to offer. Marion texted me earlier that day asking if I wanted to meet up. I agreed, and she told me when to be down at the bar. I arrived to find her with Crystal, Aaron, and Cos."

"Apart from Marion, did you know anyone at that table before that night?"

"I've met Aaron once before. I went to one of his yoga classes about a year ago, at Marion's suggestion." A small smile flittered on Rowan's lips. "I got the impression I wasn't very welcome."

"Yeah, as someone who's met Aaron, that doesn't surprise me. He probably saw you as competition to get into the pants of the women he was instructing."

"Oh good, I don't have to find a way to try to phrase that tactfully," Rowan replied, his eyes glimmering with laughter as a smile spread across his face.

"So you didn't know Crystal at all?"

"No, I'd just met her that afternoon. Marion has only been working with her for a few months."

"You're close to Marion, then?"

"It depends what you mean by close. We aren't best friends, but we keep in touch. We worked on a movie together a few years ago. It was one of my first films, in fact. Long before anyone knew my name. Marion could have ignored me completely. We were only in two scenes together, and she was Marion Hennessey, for goodness' sake. I frankly expected her to never so much as learn my name. But she did, and she gave me a pep talk one day, when I was visibly nervous before shooting an important scene. We kept in touch, and so I texted her last week when I arrived on the island."

"You're here filming a movie?"

"That's right. It's called *Sand Between my Toes.* The aim is to release it next Christmas; the studio figures in the middle of December everyone's going to want to escape with a rom-com set in Hawaii. We're here for another six weeks of shooting, and then back to LA."

"So you and Marion, there's never been any sort of tension there?"

Rowan chuckled. "Oh, no. She's great. I know a lot of people think she's stuck up, and that she thinks she's too good for anyone else, but that's just an act. In reality, when you get to know her, she's an incredibly kind person. After all, she's hired you to find Crystal's killer, when she could have just left it to the police."

"Yes, she could have."

"No, Marion is lovely in every way. She jumped right into action when Crystal fell ill too. I still can't believe it happened, really. It feels a bit like a dream. Well, a nightmare."

I nodded. "I know what you mean."

The server came by then, pen and notepad at the ready. Rowan ordered a burger and a beer, while I went for the seafood linguine.

When she left, Rowan leaned back in the booth. "So, how long have you been an investigator for?"

"Officially? Just a few months. I started back at the beginning of the year. Unofficially? A bit longer."

"I'm curious: how do you start unofficially being a private investigator?"

"When a guy gets murdered on the island and the company offers a hundred grand to anyone who helps find the killer, and you end up being that person," I replied with a grin.

Rowan let out a low whistle. "No kidding. Congratulations, that's impressive."

"That's also where the whole kidnapped-from-a-restaurant-and-driven-to-a-remote-overlook-to-be-killed thing happened."

"Crazy. So how long have you lived in Hawaii?"

"I grew up here, but I moved to Seattle as a teenager and lived there for about fifteen years."

"No kidding, I'm from Vancouver," Rowan said. "I love the Pacific Northwest."

"It was nice. I enjoyed it too," I admitted. "Still, Hawaii has my heart."

"I can understand why. This place is like no other. It's not *just* a tropical island. There's a culture here that's different to anywhere else I've ever been. The islands really feel alive, you know?"

I nodded. "I do. I know exactly what you mean."

"I also love it here. I'm thinking of getting my scuba certification on my days off."

"You should do it. I did a couple of beginner dives as a kid, and it's a lot of fun," I said with a smile. "Maui has some of the best diving spots in the world."

"So I've heard. Do you dive much?"

I shook my head. "I'm more of a 'sit on the beach and let the sun cook me until I'm a good medium-rare' type."

Rowan laughed. "Fair enough. I can't get enough of the water. I love being in it."

"The ocean is terrifying. It's deep and dark."

"So is space."

"Yeah, well, I'm not going there anytime soon, either. And you know what space doesn't have?"

"What's that?"

"Sharks."

"Space has asteroids."

"Yeah, but they follow a projected path. They're not going to chase you around the universe. If a great white sees you and thinks you're going to make a delicious meal, though, you're in trouble."

Rowan chuckled. "I can't argue with that logic. If someone gave me the option to go to space, though, I would do it. So maybe I'm just completely nuts."

"Space *and* the ocean? Yeah, you're insane."

"All the fun things in life carry risk."

"Sure. But the fun things in life don't also involve getting sand in places you didn't know existed on your body. Or being chased by fish. Or putting your foot down onto what you think is sand but is actually some sort of slimy mystery weed just waiting to wrap itself around your ankle and drag you down into the depths of hell."

"See, now I feel like you're just exaggerating. But of course, to each their own. If you don't like the water, that's cool. I'll enjoy hanging around with the lobster from *The Little Mermaid* all by myself."

"His name is Sebastian."

"Right," Rowan said with a smile. "So, if you prefer to keep your feet on dry land, what do you like doing?"

"I like walking my dog Coco on the beach," I replied, fully aware that I was not at all treating Rowan like a murder suspect anymore. But it wasn't my fault, and besides, I never knew what kind of information could lead me to finding out he was the killer.

Rowan's face brightened up immediately. "Oh! You have a dog? What breed? Do you have a picture?"

I found myself pulling out my phone and grinning as I showed Rowan a shot of Coco that I'd taken the day before. She had just inserted her snout in a hole in the sand while digging for some sort of invisible prey, and her sand-covered snoot was about an inch from the camera, her huge brown eyes in the background.

"She's adorable," Rowan said, cooing over the photo.

"She's a dachshund mixed with golden retriever. She was the runt of the litter, but she fills up my whole heart."

"I can see why."

"Do you have a dog?"

Rowan shook his head. "No. I love them. I grew up with two black labs, and they were the best. But with my work, and how often I'm away from home shooting, I can't do it right now. It wouldn't be fair to the dogs. From time to time, I foster for one of the local animal rescues in LA, if I know I'm going to be in town for a while. But these days, that's not often."

Wow. Could this guy *be* any more perfect? It wasn't enough that he was hotter than the lava under Haleakala, rich as anything, and more famous than Ryan Gosling, but he also fostered dogs when he could? He was going to have to say "down, girl!" to me, soon, if he wasn't careful.

The server arrived with our food just then, and our conversation was interrupted as we dug into our meals. Frankly, this was a good thing, because I needed to give myself another pep talk. Rowan might be a murderer. I mean, sure, I didn't really believe he was. After all, what was his motive? He didn't seem to have any reason to want Marion dead, and she had told me there was no bad blood between them, confirming his story.

The odds were Rowan was simply a friend of Marion's who just happened to be at the table when someone else tried to kill her. That said, I still had to consider him a suspect. It was possible he wanted her dead. As I'd learned in my other investigations, sometimes the motive for murder was well hidden.

Still, Rowan was disarming, and I soon found myself laughing at his jokes once more. We'd finished our meals and the plates were cleared away when someone cleared his throat next to us.

I looked over, surprised. After all, security had done a great job keeping people away from our table and allowing Rowan and me to have our conversation in private.

My eyes widened when they landed on our visitor. It was Jake.

Chapter 8

Jake's eyes darted between Rowan and me, an expression I couldn't quite read on his face. Annoyance? No, I knew that look on him *very* well. It wasn't that.

"I'm sorry, I didn't realize I was interrupting a date. I thought you were dining alone," Jake said to Rowan, a slight edge to his voice.

"This isn't a date," I said quickly. "We're just talking about the murder."

"Of course you are," Jake said, holding out a hand to Rowan, who shook it. "I'm Detective Jake Llewelyn, the primary on this case."

"Nice to meet you," Rowan said. "Charlie's right; we're just chatting about the murder."

"If that's the case, you won't mind me joining you," Jake said, sitting himself down in the booth next to me. I scowled slightly but shifted over to give him a bit more space.

"Not at all," Rowan replied, shooting me the quickest apologetic glance.

"Although that said, I really shouldn't be speaking about this in front of Charlie at all, given as she's not a member of the Maui Police Department."

"No, but I consider that a distinct advantage," I shot back at him.

"The two of you know each other, do you?" Rowan asked, an amused smile flitting on his lips.

"We're neighbors," Jake deadpanned. Was it my imagination, or was he being a little bit more brusque with Rowan than he normally would be? Whatever, I was probably overthinking it. "Now, I really do need to ask you some questions about the other day."

"Fire away." Rowan leaned comfortably back in his seat, taking another sip of his beer.

Jake glanced in my direction, and I shrugged. "Come on, we've been here an hour. I've probably already asked Rowan the questions you're about to ask, and this isn't second grade, where I'm going to cheat off your paper."

Jake considered my words for a moment. "Fine. Okay, Rowan. Did you know Crystal?"

"No. I met her for the first time that evening."

The first few questions Jake asked were basically the same ones I'd asked Rowan, but then Jake dug a little bit deeper.

"Do you have any access to Botox?"

"If you're asking whether I carry any around with me regularly, the answer is no. If you're asking whether

I could easily procure some, the answer to that is yes. I'm sure I could ask around and some of the people on set would be able to access it for me."

Jake nodded noncommittedly. "Do you know Marion's ex-husband, Bill Jamieson?"

I resisted the urge to raise my eyebrows. It appeared Jake had gotten the security camera footage and found Marion's ex-husband at the bar as well.

"I've met him," Rowan replied. "He produced my last movie. I can't say I know him well."

"Did you know he was at the bar last night?"

Rowan raised his eyebrows. "I didn't. Was he really?"

"Well, you were seated by the beach, weren't you?"

"That's right," Rowan said. "Frankly, if he arrived after we did, I never would have seen him if he stayed by the bar. And of course, after what happened with Crystal, everything became a bit of a blur. I didn't see him on my way out at all."

"What do you know about Marion and her ex-husband?"

Rowan shrugged. "I know they didn't get along. Wait, if he was there, do you think *he* might have tried to kill her?"

"What do you think?" Jake asked.

Rowan tilted his head to the side slightly as he considered the question for a moment. I couldn't help but notice the way the Edison bulbs above reflected in the light-brown shade of his eyes.

"Look, no one wants to believe they know someone

who could be a murderer," Rowan finally answered. "But without question, there was no love lost between those two. They truly hated each other, and they took their vitriol out in the press, with leaks about the other. They didn't even have to be true. You know last year, when that story came out that Bill had worked as a rent boy back in college? Well, Marion made the whole thing up. Of course, Bill turned around and threw it back onto her, saying that she had hired him, and that was how they met, because she couldn't get a date for a function. It wasn't pretty. I think... yes, I think Bill could have tried to kill her. But it was Crystal who was killed, not Marion."

"I'm just making sure that I cover all the angles. The ex-husband of a woman who's next to a murder victim just happens to be in the same bar that night? I have to investigate it, even if it turns out to have nothing to do with the crime."

"Right. Yeah, that makes sense. Sorry, don't mean to tell you how to do your job."

"There's the Canadian coming out in you," I said with a grin.

Rowan laughed. "You got it."

Jake shot me a look.

"Actually," Rowan said, snapping his fingers, "Now that you mention it, Marion told me once that Aaron uses Botox."

"Aaron Lewis, the yoga instructor?" Jake confirmed, flipping his notebook to a new page.

"That's the one. Have you met him?"

"Not yet."

I grinned. "Oh, you're in for a treat."

"I'm shocked that there's someone else on the island you didn't immediately hit it off with," Jake shot at me before turning back to Rowan. "So, Marion has told you he uses Botox for sure?"

Rowan nodded. "Yes. She'd had enough of Aaron. About a year ago, when I was here for a few days, she got me to go to one of his classes so I could see what he was about. And sure enough, I immediately understood why she'd tired of the man. As we were leaving, she told me she spotted him at a Botox clinic in town. I obviously didn't think anything of it at the time. The guy can do whatever he wants with his face, you know? But now that you're asking about it… was Crystal killed with Botox?"

"I'm afraid that's not information I'm at liberty to discuss," Jake said. But I knew the truth. Suddenly, Aaron was jumping right back up to the top of my list of suspects.

"Okay. Sorry. But, uh, yeah. I don't know if Aaron had anything against Crystal. He can't have been happy to lose Marion as a client, though."

"Thank you. Did you notice Aaron's hands near the drinks at all?" Jake's questions were short and snappy, but Rowan didn't seem to notice.

Rowan shrugged. "Honestly, the waitress put the tray down, and it was just a jumble of hands. I would have to say yes, his hands were near the drinks. They all were. But did I notice him drop anything into Crystal's? No."

"How did he seem that night? Did anyone at that table seem like they were acting strange?"

"Not to my knowledge. But then, Marion was the only person there that I knew well. Cosmic Pegasus was a little bit out there, but of course, with a name like that, I have to assume that comes with the territory. I didn't know her before that night, so I can't speak as to whether or not that was normal for her."

Jake gave a curt nod. "All right. Is there anything else you'd like to share with me before I go?"

"I don't think so," Rowan replied, hoisting a single shoulder in a shrug. "I'm afraid I don't think I know anything else that could help. But I do hope you find Crystal's killer. She seemed like a nice woman."

"Right." Jake slipped out of the booth and gave me a pointed look. "Want to join me out here?"

My eyes immediately turned to Rowan. He looked slightly bemused. Honestly, a part of me wanted to stay here and keep chatting with him. I enjoyed his company. But I also had a job to do, and I was more likely to get to the bottom of it if I went with Jake.

"Right, I'll head off as well. Thanks for dinner."

"Anytime," Rowan said easily, seemingly not taking offense to me suddenly bailing on him. I flashed him a smile then slipped out with Jake, who was already stomping back off toward the entrance.

"What was that?" I asked, struggling to catch up with him in my heels. I'd barely mastered walking—okay who was I kidding? I *definitely* hadn't mastered walking—let alone running.

"What was what?"

"This pissy mood you're in."

"I'm not in a bad mood."

"Yeah, you're a delight."

I caught up to Jake and grabbed him by the arm. "Hey."

He paused, narrowing his eyes at me. "You do realize I'm a police officer, right?"

"Yeah, and I'm obviously struggling to keep up with you. You are in a bad mood. You haven't even made fun of me for wearing heels. What's going on?"

"I'm investigating a murder, that's what's going on. And maybe I don't appreciate showing up to find my suspect already being questioned by you. Although, going by what I saw, there didn't seem to be a lot of *questioning* going on."

"Oh, is that what this is? I dare to have a little bit of fun while I'm working, and now I'm getting ignored by you? Really? Are you *that* immature?"

"He's a potential murderer, Charlie," Jake hissed, lowering his voice as he looked around.

"Do you really think that after talking to him? Besides, what was he going to do? Take a knife and stab me in the middle of that booth, where two hundred people had seen us? No. Of course he wasn't."

Jake took a deep breath. "You're right. I don't think he's the killer."

"Neither do I. And the difference between us is I'd already spent an hour with him to come to that conclusion before you came strutting in like you owned the place."

"I did not *strut*."

"Oh, you totally did."

Jake scowled in reply but didn't argue further, and I smirked at him. "Okay. So we're in agreement. Now, what do you have on the killer?"

"Absolutely not. We're not sharing information on this. I respect that you were hired by Marion to find the killer. I don't have to like it, but there's nothing I can do about it. It doesn't mean I have to tell you what I know."

"Fine. Although you know as well as I do that Marion is the ultimate target here. I get that because you get to carry a badge around that you think that makes you a more important investigator, but ultimately, isn't saving Marion's life the goal here? You told me once that you got into policing for justice. Now's your chance to prevent another murder, instead of just solving one after the fact."

We had reached the lobby by now. Jake stopped, pausing to look at me. I couldn't quite read the expression on his face. "I don't want Marion to die."

"I know you don't. Neither do I. You're pretending we're on different teams here, when really, we're on the same side."

"Are we, though?" Jake asked, a touch of acid to his voice.

Then, it hit me. "Oh, you *cannot* be jealous of Rowan. Come on. Seriously? I was hitting him up for information, and even if it was a date—which it wasn't—you have absolutely no right to give me crap for it, because we're not dating."

"I didn't mean that," Jake said, scowling slightly.

But I had a sneaking suspicion he was lying, and that caught me on my back foot a bit. Was Jake actually upset that I had been having dinner with Rowan McLeod? "When you went into this he was a suspect, Charlie. He could have killed Crystal."

"Yes, and we've been over this. I don't think he did it, and he wouldn't have killed me in the middle of the restaurant."

"Why? Because he smiled at you and bought you dinner?" There was that salty version of Jake again.

"No, wise-ass, because he doesn't have a motive. Come on. I can help you with this. I'm not asking you for crime scene access, or for you to run fingerprints for me. I'm just saying, if the two of us talk this over a bit, we have a better chance of figuring it out and saving Marion's life. Isn't that ultimately what we all want?"

"I already have someone I can talk things over with. I have a partner, remember?"

"Liam? I mean, no offense to him, but that's like having a conversation with a French fry."

"I don't see how that could possibly be taken as anything other than offensive."

"Okay, fine. I did mean the offense. But my point stands. Talk to me. Tell me what you know, and I'll tell you what I've found out. Between us, we have an opportunity to save a woman's life. Don't you want to close this case with one body in the morgue instead of two?"

Jake breathed in deep, then finally nodded.

"You're right. I do. Okay, let's get out of here."

I smiled to myself as Jake turned and headed

toward the exit, strutting after him for about two steps before I misplaced a high heel and just about sprained my ankle.

"Stupid shoes," I muttered under my breath as I followed after him.

Chapter 9

I rode along with Jake as we drove back to Kihei, ending up at Moose McGillycuddy's right on South Kihei Road. This wasn't the fancy five-star resort bar and restaurant I'd just come from. Here, chipped wooden tables with painted green tops were surrounded by tall mahogany chairs, the stain on the edges having worn away. At least twenty big screen TVs around the room showed every sporting event currently underway in the world, by the looks, and above the bar hung pennants from all the NFL teams. Every inch of wall space was covered with framed photos, and high up in the rafters an Edmonton Oilers flag hung below a BC Lions T-shirt and a green-and-white flag with an "S" on it that I didn't recognize.

"Saskatchewan Roughriders," Jake said, noticing my gaze. "Canadian football."

"Well gee, how silly of me to not have recognized *that*," I said, and Jake laughed as a friendly-looking woman approached us. She led us to a booth, the seating made of plain wood, and handed us a couple of menus.

After thanking her, Jake grinned at me. "Well, it's not the Maui Diamond Resort, but hopefully it'll do."

"I've never actually been here," I said, perusing the menu. It was full of bright colors and comfort food, with some delicious-looking cocktail options.

"This is a great place. A real feeling of aloha. I love it here. The food is great, the beer is cold, the people are friendly. What more can you ask for?"

"That's pretty much it," I said as the server came by. I ordered a lava flow—a pina colada with strawberry purée—and Jake went for a beer on tap. When the server left, he leaned back against the hard wood of the booth.

"So, what are you thinking with this case?" he asked.

"I think Marion is right about her being the intended target. Given what she's told me about that night, she was supposed to drink that pina colada. It wasn't meant for Crystal. Do you agree?"

Jake paused for a moment, as if considering whether or not to reply. After all, if he did, he was crossing that line into sharing insights into his investigation with someone who wasn't a cop. And I knew that was going to be a big moment for him.

But I also knew that above everything, as much as I gave him crap for being annoying, he wanted to get justice for Crystal, and he didn't want a second body to land in his lap. So, he answered. "Yes, I agree. I think

Marion was the real target, and whoever tried to kill her might do so again. So, who do you think did it?"

"Right now, Aaron Lewis is at the top of my suspect list. Although, Marion's ex-husband being at the bar on the night in question is certainly suspicious. You knew he was there at the same time as Marion's group?"

"Yes. We saw the security footage. How did *you* know?"

I coughed into my hand. "Uh, maybe that's not something I'm going to admit in front of a member of law enforcement."

Jake narrowed his eyes at me. "Seriously? You stole it?"

"I didn't say that."

"This was a bad idea."

"No, it's actually an excellent idea. And you know what I think? I think it would be an enormous coincidence if Marion's ex-husband just *happened* to stop the waitress taking the drinks to Marion's table to ask her something and didn't have anything to do with the murder. But at the same time, if he *did* do it, it was very brazen. It's not like they hide the fact that there are security cameras in that place. What's the point of killing someone if you're going to get caught almost immediately?"

"Luckily for me, that's actually what happens most of the time. Most murders aren't sexy mysteries that make great stories to tell in books. They're spur-of-the-moment attacks by people who haven't thought through the consequences of what's going to happen to them."

"In this case, though, the killer had to know what they were going to do ahead of time. I mean, sure, this isn't Hollywood, but I'd be willing to bet Bill Jamieson doesn't make a habit of wandering around with vials of Botox in his back pocket just in case the chance to poison his ex-wife comes up," I pointed out. "So, if it was premeditated—and I think this one has to be—then why do it in a restaurant with security cameras? Why not put in just a little bit more effort to try to actually get away with it?"

"That's a very good point," Jake said, idly running a finger along the edge of the abandoned lime sitting next to his drink.

I smiled as warmth flooded through my body at Jake's praise. Okay, so maybe I liked it when Jake recognized I was a good investigator. At least, that was what I told myself I cared about.

"The problem is, that takes us back to it being a coincidence. You saw the same video I did. His hands just happened to be out of view of the camera. I don't like that. I don't like it at all. Have you spoken to him yet?"

"Bill?"

I nodded.

"No," Jake said with a shake of his head. "Haven't had the chance to. I'm going to see him tomorrow morning."

"How early tomorrow?"

Jake shot me an askance look. "Why do you want to know?"

"Because my shift at Aloha Ice Cream starts at

ten?" I offered with a grin. "I just thought maybe if it was early enough, I could pop in and give you a hand, you know?"

"You're impossible. You do realize that, don't you? I'm willing to talk to you about this case, because you've legitimately been hired to find the killer, and I think it could help, but there is no way I'm going to have you join in an official police interview."

"You're such a buzzkill," I replied, taking another sip of my drink.

"A buzzkill who likes having a job."

"If you think I'm going to report you to your boss, you're in luck. I don't even know who your boss is."

"It's not you I'm worried about. Besides, there's nothing to discuss here. End of story. If you want to interview Bill Jamieson on your own time, you're welcome to do that. I don't have the right to complain about it anymore. But you're not a cop, and you can't come to my interview."

"Fine," I replied. "I'll talk to him on my own."

"I saw you're famous now too. TMZ?"

I groaned. "Yeah. They could have picked a more flattering picture."

"I thought you looked cute," Jake said, before quickly continuing. "Anyway, that's got to be good for your business."

"I hope so," I said, glossing over the cute comment. What did he mean by that? Was he just being nice? Of course he was. But I never really thought of Jake as being nice for the sake of it. Annoying, sure. Frustrating? Absolutely. Funny? Okay, sometimes. But nice? I didn't quite know how to react to that. "It felt weird, though. Still feels weird. It's like it's not real, in a way. I mean, me? On the TMZ website? That's not something I could have ever imagined. But then, I load it up, and there I am, having coffee with freaking Marion Hennessey. And she's hiring me for a job."

"Yup. I can see how that would mess with you a bit. But hey, she hired you for a reason. You were already one of the highest-profile investigators on the island, thanks to the James MacMahon case."

"I guess. But there's a difference between my picture being in *The Maui News* and TMZ."

"True. Listen, Charlie. I want you to be careful out there." I was just tensing my eye muscles, getting ready to roll them, when Jake continued. "I know I can't tell you not to investigate this case anymore. I have no standing. You're an investigator; you've been hired to do a job. I might not like it, but you're a grown woman who can make her own decisions, even if I think sometimes a toddler thinks things through more than you do."

Okay, I had a track record of not making the best life decisions, so I couldn't really argue against that one. Still, I was figuring it out.

Jake continued. "But the thing is, whoever killed Crystal is still out there, and still wants Marion Hennessey dead. You're now publicly investigating this murder for her, which means one of two things: either the killer is going to decide there's way too much heat on them and they're going to lay low for a while, or they're going to strike again, and fast. If you're near her, you're a potential target."

"I've considered that. Frankly, it's a risk I think is worth taking. I like Marion. I mean, we'll never be best friends or anything, but I don't think she deserves to die."

"Neither do I. But you don't deserve to die, either."

"I'll do my best not to," I said, flashing Jake a cheeky smile. "Now, tell me, and be honest: how many posters of Marion Hennessey did you have on your wall growing up?"

Jake burst out laughing. "Honest answer? None. She wasn't really my type. I was all about the heroines in my favorite movies. Now, Carrie Fischer as Princess Leia? *That* was my favorite poster. She was a total badass, and she looked super hot in that gold bikini. How about you? Who adorned your childhood walls?"

"Indiana Jones," I replied with a nostalgic smile. "He was a favorite of both mine and Zoe's. She loved how he was an archaeologist who went on adventures, and I loved how cool he was. And of course, the scene where he shot the guy with the sword."

Jake chuckled. "You know, I'm not sure what answer I was expecting, but I'm not surprised by that one. If I swung the other way, I probably would have had Han Solo on my wall instead."

"Sadly, no one is out there trying to kill Harrison Ford, so I don't think I'm going to get to meet him. Although I did learn that one of the other people who lives in our building may or may not have had an affair with him back in the eighties."

Jake raised an eyebrow. "Let me guess: Vesper?"

"Got it in one. Think she's telling the truth?" I asked with a grin.

Jake paused, biting his lower lip slightly as he considered the question. "I think it could go either way. She's told me some outrageous stories before. About a year ago, Vesper told me that in the early eighties she was kidnapped by drug dealers because her boyfriend at the time owed them money, and that she managed to get away and blow up their entire operation because she learned how to make explosives in her high school chemistry class. I'm still, like, ninety percent sure that story isn't true, but I did look into it and found that a drug den exploded in eighty-two, killing four known dealers. It was chalked up as an accident, though, and Vesper's name never showed up in the report. But it's not like she would have stuck around."

I chuckled. "Or, she could have just heard about the explosion happening, and decided to make a good story out of it."

"Right. There's no way of knowing for sure. So, no, I don't know if she's telling the truth about Harrison Ford."

"Personally, I choose to believe all her crazy stories. Life is more fun when you think you have a neighbor who once stowed away in a container ship to get to a surfing competition on the mainland because she didn't have the money for a plane ticket."

Jake laughed. "She's certainly got some stories to tell. Anyway, I hope this case doesn't end up as interesting as Vesper's life. I don't want you getting hurt. I know I can't tell you to stay out of it, but I want you to be careful, Charlie. I mean it."

"I will be," I said. "I don't go looking for trouble."

"And yet somehow it always manages to find you."

"Sure, but that's not on me."

"You might not think so, but everyone else on this island manages to go more than a week without being Tasered."

"Please. That's only happened to me a few times."

"That's a few more than everyone else you know, except me."

I raised my eyebrows. "You've had it happen to you? Let me guess, your idiot partner thought you were a criminal one day because you wore your pants a little low."

"No. They made us all get Tasered when we started using them so we'd know what it felt like. I guess the higher-ups thought it would make us less likely to use them willy-nilly if we knew how awful it felt."

"Liam didn't get the message," I muttered. "So, how long have you been a cop for? It must be a while."

"I feel as if I've just been called old."

"Ever since I saw a tweet from a teenager asking why we say 'picking up the phone,' I've felt like I belong in a nursing home."

Jake groaned. "I would have been happier not knowing that. Anyway, I was in the Navy. Then I went to UH to study engineering, but I left after a family emergency in my second year. I decided I wanted to help people again, and I ended up becoming a police officer."

"I'm sorry," I said quietly, thinking that this probably wasn't the time to ask for details. "For the family emergency thing. Not the fact that you became a cop. Well, maybe a little bit of that. Engineers help people. I like being able to drive on roads that don't collapse into the ocean."

Jake laughed. "I would have designed the best roads you'd ever seen."

"You could have designed the highway between Upcountry and Wailea that they'll never build."

"Hey, if we're lucky, one day the state will buy the private one Oprah built a few years ago."

I grinned. "You think she'll let it go?"

"Probably not," Jake admitted. "But seeing as they've been talking about building a road through there my entire life and she's the only one who's made it happen so far, I'm not getting my hopes up."

"Fair enough."

The conversation continued, and before I knew it, the restaurant was closing up for the night. Jake and I paid for our drinks and left, and we hailed a cab back to our apartment complex, just to be on the safe side. As I said goodnight to him and continued down the hall to my place, I tried to ignore the warm and fuzzy feeling inside of me.

"So, are you sure I can't come along when you interview Bill Jamieson tomorrow?" I asked Jake with a grin as he entered his apartment.

"Good night, Charlie."

Chapter 10

I woke up with a pounding headache the next morning and fixed it with a breakfast of Advil and Tater Tots. Zoe wasn't home; I figured she was at the hospital, working, so I was free to eat my breakfast of champions without her judgement.

After a quick walk along the beach with Coco—the fresh sea air and rhythmic lapping of the waves against the shore certainly helped move the headache along as well—I got ready for my shift at Aloha Ice Cream.

Unfortunately, Queenie was still parked at the Maui Diamond Resort, and I figured I should probably rescue my Jeep before she got towed.

Luckily, when I got to the resort, Queenie was still there in all her neon-blue glory, and I started her up before pulling back onto South Kihei Road and joining the stream of traffic going north. With the roof down and the wind blowing in my hair, my sunglasses cutting through the glare of the sun, I wondered how I had ever made it through a single dreary Seattle winter, where I used to joke that the sun was taking a yearly sabbatical between the months of October and April.

It was the first week of March now, and the winter weather was slowly starting to warm up. The humpback whales that had been so commonly seen offshore during their yearly migration the past months were now fewer in number, and soon they would be gone entirely, heading back to Alaska and their summer home.

The winter tourists were leaving along with them, and we'd get a few months of lower numbers before they began visiting in droves once more in the summer months when kids were off from school.

Still, that didn't stop traffic from being awful all over the island, and by the time I found a parking spot and wandered into Aloha Ice Cream, I was a few minutes late for the start of my shift.

"Sorry, traffic was awful," I said to Leslie as I walked in. Luckily, she'd just opened, and it didn't appear that we had any customers yet.

"No worries," she replied. Leslie was a no-nonsense business owner with a bandana holding back her mousy-brown hair from her face. She was elbow deep in a container of passionfruit hibiscus sorbet, getting the last few scoops and putting them on top of a new container to replace it. "I saw you're famous now. Is it true you're investigating the death of that yoga instructor?"

I nodded. "Sure is. It's a real tragedy."

"So, what's Marion Hennessey like in real life? She's always exuded so much class. Even when she divorced that good-for-nothing husband of hers. Please don't tell me she's actually an awful person."

I laughed. "No, don't worry. She's not awful. In fact, I kind of like her. She's very guarded, but I don't blame her for that. I think I would be, too, if every facet of my life was put under a microscope for investigation. But beneath that Kevlar exterior, she seems nice. She obviously cares about the people in her life, even if they aren't as rich and famous as she is."

"That's good to hear. I always thought she was such a gifted actress, and I've been a big fan of hers for years. You never want to hear that your heroes are actually horrible people."

"Well, in this case, I think you're safe."

"Good. What was it like, seeing your picture on TMZ?"

I grimaced. "Well, first of all, if I'd known that was going to happen, I would have worn something nicer. And maybe tried to look a little bit less like a hippo who just spent the morning devouring a watermelon."

Leslie burst out laughing. "Oh, come on. I know we're always harder on ourselves than anyone else is, but you looked fine."

"I didn't. It was one of the most unflattering pictures of myself that I've ever seen. And Zoe once took a picture of me coming out of the water after snorkeling where I literally looked like Cthulhu had grown legs and was coming ashore. But at least hundreds of thousands of people never saw that picture. It lives in Zoe's phone, where she threatens to show it to people if I'm being mean to her, and that's it. But she never will. She's too nice for that."

"I think you're being way too hard on yourself."

"Trust me, if you had your picture taken next to Marion Hennessey looking like a supermodel drinking a latte between shoots, you'd be hard on yourself too. Anyway, I have taken her case. I want to find the person who killed Crystal."

"It's very sad. Who would do something like that?"

"Well, that's what I want to find out. Hey, you tried to get me to do yoga once, didn't you?"

A small smiled flittered on Leslie's lips. "I believe I've mentioned it to you once or twice as an option."

"Do you know an Aaron Lewis, or Cosmic Pegasus?"

Leslie rolled her eyes. "Yes to both. Cos is a lovely thing, beautiful soul inside and out. Aaron is one of the slimiest people I've ever met, though. He's one of those asses who doesn't actually appreciate the art of yoga, but simply sees it as a way to make money, and to get into women's pants."

"That's pretty much exactly the vibe I got from him. I was thinking of going to see Cosmic Pegasus later today."

"You should. She has classes most afternoons. Check her Instagram to see where she's running them today. They're usually at Kamaole I, unless the winds are too high."

"Winds?" I asked. "What does that have to do with yoga?"

"Cos's classes are all done on stand-up paddleboards."

I let out a groan. "Right. I knew that, and I think I repressed the memory because it sounded so horrifying. Yoga is hard enough on solid land. You want to throw in floating on a 30-inch-wide glorified surfboard in the middle of the ocean?"

"You're in a protected cove, not the open ocean. Besides, it works your stabilizer muscles, and improves your balance."

"Great. I guess that's what I'll be doing this afternoon. You wouldn't happen to have a paddleboard I can borrow, do you?"

"Of course. Mine's inflatable, too, so you can just throw it in the back of your Jeep and pump it up when you get there."

"Thanks, Leslie. I appreciate it."

Our first few customers of the day began meandering into the store, and for the next couple of hours, I was focused entirely on waffle cones and sundaes.

The lunch rush was just coming to an end when a woman walked in, looking lost. Her navy-blue shorts and pink blouse were obviously designer wear, and a large Prada tote hung from her arm. Now, this wasn't exactly a rare sight in Hawaii. We got a lot of high-end tourists, but they were more often found in Wailea than up here in the quiet, more local community of Kihei.

Looking to be in her late forties, the woman's shoulder-length blond hair was tidy, in a perfect coiffe, which was incredibly impressive in the Maui heat. Usually by the time noon came around, my hair was plastered against my neck and my bangs had taken on a life of their own. Her blue eyes scanned the room, but the bloodshot whites and slightly puffy skin below betrayed that she'd been crying.

"Can I help you?" I asked cautiously. I was a firm believer that no matter what your problem, triple-chocolate-chunk ice cream could make it at least a little bit better, though this woman looked like she was going to need a gallon of it.

"Are you Charlie Gibson?" the woman asked. "I was told she works here."

"That's me," I replied.

"Thank God. You have to help me. My husband has disappeared." Her voice cracked on the last word, and she burst into tears, burying her face in her hands.

"Okay. First things first: ice cream. Let me grab you a cup, and we're going to sit down at that table over there, and you're going to tell me all about it from start to finish."

The commanding tone in my voice seemed to help, and the woman nodded. She walked over to the table that I motioned toward and plopped herself down on the chair. Leslie was out the back, and I called for her to take over for a minute, scooping ice cream into a cup for the woman and sticking a compostable spoon in the top.

I sat across from the woman and pushed the cup of ice cream toward her. "All right. Tell me about your husband."

"His name is John. John Waters."

"And what's your name?"

"Vanessa. We've been married for twenty-two years. We were high school sweethearts. Married at nineteen. Our daughter left for college just a few months ago, in September. She's at Stanford. Charlie, you have to help me. I don't know where he is."

"Okay. When was the last time you saw John?"

"Two days ago, in the morning. He left for work, like he always did. Kissed me goodbye, told me to have a nice day. Grabbed his phone and wallet off the hall stand, and off he went. That night, when he didn't come home, I called him. I phoned so many times, but I never heard back. I called the police, and they told me that I'd have to wait until he was missing for forty-eight hours before they could file a missing persons report. I called my daughter, Ellie. I wasn't going to. I didn't want her to worry. But I also needed to know if she'd heard from John. She hadn't, but told me to find you. Ellie said you were a private investigator, and that you worked with famous people. You had a good reputation. I looked you up online, and saw that you worked at Aloha Ice Cream when you solved the James MacMahon case. So I came here today on the chance you were still here. I'm so glad you are. I'll pay you anything. Just please, find my husband. Will you help me?"

This was going to be my first missing person case. I really, desperately, hoped that John Waters had just had a few too many after work and was sleeping it off in a ditch somewhere.

"I will," I replied. "You say he was acting normally when he went to work yesterday. What about in the days and weeks leading up to that? Was there anything out of the ordinary going on?"

"No," Vanessa said, shaking her head. "I know what you're thinking. But no. John wouldn't have hurt himself. Or worse. Everything was fine. We were fine. He was normal."

"Where does he work?"

"He's a lawyer at one of the firms in Kahului. Leman, Horowitz and Chalmers. That's the other weird thing. I called them this morning, and they told me he doesn't work there anymore. But they can't be right. John's been going to work every single day. I didn't know what to do. He works there; I know he does."

Vanessa's eyes, filled with desperation, implored me to find her answers. Her ice cream sat untouched in front of her, a melted glob beginning to slide down the side of the cup.

"Leave it with me," I told her. "I'll see what I can find out, and I'll call you tonight, okay?"

Vanessa nodded. "You'll find him?"

"I will," I replied, cringing inwardly. I knew I wasn't supposed to guarantee people results. Every TV show on the planet had taught me that, and yet the words came out of my mouth anyway. Why was I like this?

"Thank you, Charlie. To be honest, I wasn't one hundred percent sure about hiring you. I thought maybe I should just wait for the police to find him. But… I'm worried. I really am. It's not like John to do anything like this. He's always come home. Always. He's never cheated on me. We're happy. I stayed at home and raised Ellie, and he provided a very good living for us. We didn't have problems. We didn't have secrets. Something is wrong. I can feel it in my bones."

"Where can I reach you?"

Vanessa pulled her phone from her purse, her hand trembling slightly, and we traded contact information. When we were finished, Vanessa took the spoon from the cup of ice cream and had a bite.

"Thank you. I already feel better, knowing you're on this case."

"Of course. Listen, you sit here and finish this ice cream, okay? It'll make you feel better. Then go home, and I don't know, maybe try to get some sleep. I'll be in touch."

"Thank you."

I had another client to take care of.

Chapter 11

My shift at Aloha Ice Cream ended at three, but Cosmic Pegasus's stand-up paddleboard yoga class wasn't until five thirty. With the sun setting just around an hour later than that these days, that would allow us to enjoy the evening with the last few rays of the sun shining down on us.

It would have been romantic if it weren't for the part that involved paddleboarding. Or yoga.

I decided to spend the time I had before the yoga session looking into John Waters's life. It was curious, what Vanessa had said about him not working at the law firm. I hadn't pushed her on that point. Vanessa was obviously already overwhelmed, but it was a good place for me to start.

After hopping into Queenie, I looked up Leman, Horowitz and Chalmers, plugged the address into Google Maps, and started driving as the robotic voice told me where to go. The building housing the firm was located in Wailuku, in a structure that could best be described as seventies concrete chic. Plain, beige, and four stories tall, I parked on the street below, entered, and followed the signs to the third floor.

I entered the offices of Leman, Horowitz and Chalmers to find myself in a much more modern-looking space. Unlike the exterior of the building, this interior had definitely met a designer's hand sometime this century.

Cool gray-white marble tiles on the floor were matched beautifully with an enormous warm wood desk that dominated the reception area. Behind it was a fabric accent wall printed with the name of the firm in gold lettering. On either side were a couple of reception areas, where leather upholstered chairs dotted glass tables sprinkled with the latest issues of about ten different magazines.

In the corner, a plumeria plant bloomed in a modern, black square pot.

Behind the desk, a woman in her thirties, her blond hair hanging down to her shoulders, spoke into a headset, holding up a single finger along with a polite smile, indicating to me that I should wait a moment. I stood back from the desk until she ended her call and turned her attention to me.

"Hello, how can I help you?"

"I'm Charlie Gibson, an investigator working on behalf of Vanessa Waters, trying to find her husband."

The woman at reception pursed her lips, and her voice got noticeably cooler when she spoke. "Oh, yes. She called this morning about him."

"Vanessa told me you said her husband no longer works here?"

"He was let go about six months ago. He hasn't worked here in that long, and I'm not sure why she believed he was still under our employ. Of course, if he was the kind of man who didn't tell his wife he wasn't working at the firm, he's probably the kind of man who wouldn't tell her where he goes at night, either." The woman gave me a look that screamed that she wasn't particularly sympathetic to Vanessa Waters's plight, and that she'd perhaps brought it on herself.

"Why was he laid off?"

"I'm afraid that's confidential information."

"Look, I honestly don't care about the answer beyond finding the guy. I have reason to believe he might be in real trouble, and that this isn't just a clueless wife who doesn't realize her husband is doing the dance with no pants somewhere else. This information might be the difference between finding him alive, and giving Vanessa a body to bury. I promise, no one will find out this information came from you, but I need to know what happened."

The receptionist's eyes widened. "You really think he might be dead?"

"I do," I lied, trying to look as serious as possible. Okay, it was possible he was bleeding to death in a ditch, but frankly, I had no real reason to believe that just yet.

The receptionist took a deep breath, biting her lower lip, obviously trying to decide what to do.

"It could save his life," I implored, trying to get her over that line, and it worked.

"Alright," she finally said, looking around furtively as if the walls might listen in. "But you didn't hear this from me."

I made a zipping motion across my lips.

"His work had started slipping. He lost a few cases that should have been gimmes. I think he was burned out. It happens, in this environment. Law is a space where forty-hour weeks are virtually unheard of, and John just wasn't cutting it. He was the sort of lawyer who would never make partner; he wasn't good enough for that. He had reached his ceiling, stayed there for a while, and was burning out. The partners had to let someone go, and his number was up. But why didn't his wife know?"

I shrugged. "No idea. Probably one of those guys whose entire ego is wrapped up in the pride he takes in his work, and he was too embarrassed to tell her. Still, going out and pretending to work every day for six months is some dedication. That lady loves him more than anything. I'm pretty sure she would have been fine with it if he was temporarily out of work."

The receptionist shrugged. "All I know is he was given a small severance package."

"What would his financial situation have looked like, overall? I'm not asking for specifics, just give me a general idea of what a non-partner lawyer might make."

"A decent living, for sure. More than I'm ever going to make. Maybe a hundred and fifty grand?"

I let out a low whistle. "Not too shabby. I should have considered law school after all."

"No kidding. Although personally, I like being out of here at five every night. Anyway, I can't help you with anything else. Do you think this will help you find John?"

"I do. You didn't seem to be the biggest fan of his."

The receptionist shrugged. "It isn't that I think he's a bad guy. I just wouldn't know one way or the other. He was a male lawyer, fifteen years older than me, who happened to work in the same office I do. I don't consider my coworkers to be my friends. I consider them people I have to be around for eight hours a day so I get paid. I hope he's not dead, but beyond that, it's like learning the guy in line in front of you at the coffee shop disappeared. Sure, that sucks, but you move on with your life."

Damn. It was cold, but I had to respect her honesty. I'd had a few coworkers over the years where if they disappeared, I'd have had to pretend to be sad about it, but I certainly would have pretended. Even if they'd been laid off half a year earlier. Apparently, this lady just didn't have time for that.

"Is there anyone here he might have been close to? Confided in?"

"I don't think so. John was never the sociable type. And he's been gone from here a while. I haven't heard anyone mention staying in touch."

"Okay, thanks."

I headed back down to the street, thinking about what I'd just learned. John Waters was an average lawyer who had burned out but was too embarrassed to tell his wife. At least, that was what it sounded like. What it did mean, however, was that money was probably tight. A hundred and fifty grand a year was a great income, for sure, but it wasn't life-changing, either. Not on Maui, where the average home cost over a million dollars and mainlanders had to be warned about the sticker shock they'd experience at the grocery store.

How on earth had he been making money for the last six months?

I pulled out my phone and dialed Dot's number.

"Hey, Charlie. What's up? How was your dinner with Rowan? Got a lead on your killer yet?"

"No, but I have a new case, and I'm wondering if you can dig up some information for me while I go to stand-up paddleboard yoga. The meeting went well. I'll tell you about it later, but the short version is I don't think he's the killer, and Rowan's pretty nice."

"I'll only help if you take video of the yoga class for me, because it sounds like it's going to be hilarious."

"If by hilarious you mean embarrassing and humiliating, I think you're on the right track."

"Well, one person's humiliating is another person's entry into *America's Funniest Home Videos*."

"Is that even on TV anymore?"

"If not, it should be. So, what's the name?"

"John Waters."

"What a boring name. He sounds like a lawyer."

"He *is* a lawyer."

Dot cackled on the other end of the line, pleased

with her own brilliant guess. "Are you looking for anything specific on him?"

"His finances. He's gone missing, and his wife is worried. It turns out he got let go from his job six months ago, and he hadn't told her."

"So, you're wondering how he's managed to keep afloat in that time?"

"Exactly. Also, if you find anything that indicates he might have used a credit or debit card recently, or used his phone, that would be handy too. I get the feeling his wife isn't exactly up-to-date on their finances."

"Got it. I'll get back to you in a few hours."

"Thanks, Dot. You're the best. I'll come by after my yoga class."

"Don't forget that video," Dot teased on the other end of the line.

That was all I needed. The entire world seeing me try a downward-facing dog on a unstable board in the middle of the ocean. I had a sneaking suspicion it was going to look more like an upward-facing baby elephant on cocaine.

Chapter 12

I stopped by Leslie's place on the way back and let myself into her garage—she had given me the entry code back at the ice cream shop—and found the bag containing her inflatable stand-up paddleboard. I hoisted it up into the front seat and drove down to Ulua Beach, the site of today's stand-up tortureboard yoga session. I had signed up online earlier.

Ulua Beach was located in Wailea, right in the heart of some of the most expensive hotel rooms and suites on the island.

Finding a spot in the public parking lot, I changed into a bathing suit—this being Maui, I always had one in the back of the car just in case—and pulled the paddleboard from the bag, rolled it out onto the road, and began inflating it.

"Easy, my ass," I panted after five minutes of continuous pumping. I was already sweating, and I hadn't even done any exercise, yet. Eventually, however, the pump read that I'd gotten the board to 12 PSI, and I was ready to go.

I awkwardly carried the board under one arm, with the paddle in the other as I headed down to the beach. Small by Maui standards, Ulua Beach was only a couple hundred yards long, but that didn't diminish its beauty.

Dotted on either side by black lava fields that stood out strikingly against the turquoise blue of the ocean, soft waves beat white against the rocks every few seconds. The back of the beach was lined with bushes and manicured gardens, a path meandering along the length of it, dotted with tall palm trees that swayed in the light breeze.

On the golden sand, couples and families sat on folding chairs or lay spread out on towels. Children shrieked with joy as they played in the surf, though the waves crashing on the beach were fairly smooth this afternoon. No wonder Cosmic Pegasus had chosen this spot for today's class; the water turned glassy only a few feet out from shore.

Thank goodness for small mercies.

I walked toward the water and placed the board on the sand, leaning against it, wondering how on earth I was going to do this. I had never paddle-boarded in my life. I know, I was the worst Hawaiian ever *and* the worst Seattleite ever. But I needed to get a read on Cosmic Pegasus, and hopefully some information, and this was the best way to do it.

"You must be here for my class," a voice said

behind me. I turned and found myself looking at a woman who could *only* be Cosmic Pegasus.

Her hair had been dyed strawberry blond and cascaded along her front in soft waves, with streaks of blues, pinks and purples running through it. In the corner of a woven leather headband was a pink hibiscus flower. She wore matching harem pants and a brown sports bra, and a purple crystal hung from a plain leather strap around her neck. She leaned a fancy-looking paddleboard against her side.

"I am," I said. "I'm Charlie."

"Call me Cos. You're working for Marion to find Crystal's killer, may her soul find peace, aren't you?"

"Yes. I was hoping I could ask you some questions about that night."

"Of course you can. Whatever you need, I'm at your service. Crystal had a beautiful spirit, and it's such a tragedy that the universe decided she needed to be taken from us so soon. I wear an amethyst crystal today, as it's a healer of the mind and spirit, and a stone that offers release. I've been using it to help release the pain I feel knowing that Crystal is gone forever, and the anger I feel toward the person who took her life."

Well, I couldn't exactly claim that I was *surprised* that the hippie yoga instructor named Cosmic Pegasus was one of those people who thought crystals had magical properties, but I still didn't really know what to reply to that, so I ignored it and moved on.

"Can you run me through what happened that night?"

"I was having drinks with Aaron Lewis. A mutual friend set us up."

"How was it going between the two of you?"

Cos scrunched up her face. "Let's just say he wasn't my type, and I wasn't his. I knew his reputation, of course. He's known in some of the local yogi circles as being more interested in the money it's possible to earn on the backs of lonely women than he is his interest in the spiritual practice. However, I am not one to take gossip at face value, and I thought it only fair to give the man the benefit of the doubt. Unfortunately, it became quickly obvious as we began to speak that Aaron truly believes in one true higher power: himself."

I laughed. "That's exactly the impression I got. Was that your first date, then?"

"It was, yes."

Interesting. Aaron had told me he had been seeing Cos casually, not that it was their first date. Was he just trying to make himself sound like less of a loser who was totally bombing with the woman he'd been set up with, or was there more to the story?

Cos continued. "Frankly, I'd already had four drinks by the time Marion and Crystal walked past. I'm not normally much of a drinker, but I'd tried all of my meditation strategies, and I couldn't help but feel more and more distaste for Aaron every time he opened his mouth. So, I turned to alcohol. I figured if I was lucky, I'd have no memory of the night at all. Then, I spotted Crystal and Marion walking through the restaurant. Aaron must have seen this as his chance to show off his acquaintance with someone famous, as he waved them both over, emphasizing the fact that he knew Marion Hennessey. I spoke to Crystal for a little bit, and I was thrilled they accepted his invitation to join us, though."

"Aaron was the one who invited them to sit?"

"Yes. Crystal sat next to me, and Marion across from her. Aaron struck up a conversation with Marion, and I confided in Crystal that the date wasn't going well. She sympathized with me. Then, a few minutes later, Rowan McLeod showed up. To be honest, when we were a crowd, I didn't think things were too bad. It was nice, being able to speak with the others. I could almost forget Aaron was there. Then, the drinks arrived, Crystal switched with Marion, had a sip of hers, and immediately collapsed. It was awful."

"Had you met Marion before that night?"

"No," Cos replied. "I knew she was a customer of Aaron's for a while, and Crystal's more recently, but I'd never met her myself."

"Did you hear anything at that table that might make you think someone else who was there might have wanted to hurt her?"

Cos's eyes widened just slightly, and her mouth made an 'o' shape. "The drink swap. You think Marion was the target. Crystal wasn't supposed to die."

"It's only a theory at the moment," I said carefully. "For Marion's safety, I don't want it getting out."

"I understand completely. You don't have to worry about me. I will guard this secret with all of my power. There has been one needless death already; I have no intention to bring about a second."

"Thank you," I said. "Now, did you hear anything that might tell you who wanted Marion dead?"

Cos bit her lip as she considered the question, but shook her head. "No. Not a thing. The mood at the table was jovial. Certainly much more so than when it was only Aaron and me. I can't think of a thing that might help. Sorry."

"Did Marion mention her ex-husband at all?"

Cos frowned slightly. "No. Why would she?"

"Just a question, that's all. All right, thank you. I think that's everything."

If I was lucky, I might even get out of having to do yoga. I'd already gotten all the answers I needed.

"Wonderful. You're still going to stay for the session, right?"

"Well, actually—" I started, but Cos interrupted me.

"You should stay. Come, and spend an hour on the water with me. You're already here, and you have your board. What is stopping you?"

"I've never done yoga before, for one. Or paddle-boarding."

"Then what better day to start than today? We were all beginners at one point, and I will take you through a flow that will align your chakras and have you feeling refreshed and reinvigorated."

"My chakras seem pretty aligned to me already," I replied. "Besides, I promise I'll do a bit of a hamstring stretch when I get home."

Cos flashed me a cheeky smile. "You seem to me to be the kind of woman who takes chances in life. Take a chance on this class. Or have I got you all wrong, and you're the type to run back off to your car and hide?"

Ugh. Great. Cos had picked me perfectly. I wasn't going to fall for this chakra alignment crap, but call me a coward for not daring to do the class, and I was basically guaranteed to do it out of spite.

My stupid lizard brain would do anything to prove her wrong. Why was I like this?

"All right, fine," I heard myself saying. "I'll do the class. Let's go."

"Great," Cos replied, turning and motioning for me to follow her. "We're just about to start."

I followed after Cos and mentally crossed her off my list of suspects for now. After all, she had no motive. By all accounts, she'd never met Marion Hennessey before, and barring a lie on her part, that meant she'd have no reason to want her dead, unless she was some sort of Manson-like serial killer, but with better hair.

And if Cos didn't know about Bill Jamieson being at the bar, I had to infer that it wasn't discussed at all. That made it even more likely that none of them knew about his being there. Someone would have mentioned it if they had. I couldn't help but wonder what Jake had found out that morning while interviewing the man.

That was going to have to wait until after this session. If I didn't drown, anyway.

Cos waded out into the water until it came about halfway up her shins, then she placed the board down. It was deep enough that the fins on the bottom didn't scrape against the sand, and she deftly climbed up onto it, standing easily and beginning to paddle out into the more open water.

"Okay, here goes nothing," I muttered to myself as I tried to imitate her. I placed my board down, and I was suddenly *very* aware of how much it was moving, even in the protected waters of the small bay. I placed a single leg on the board, right in the middle, and tried to stand.

The board immediately jetted out from underneath me, and I let out a yelp as I suddenly found myself doing the splits into the water. I immediately fell sideways, my hamstrings not nearly flexible enough to handle what I was trying to do, and the next thing I knew, I was sitting on the sand, spitting out a mouthful of salt water.

Then, because the universe hadn't shit on me enough these last fifteen seconds or so, a wave broke over my head, covering me with even more salt water.

Zoe was the one who enjoyed this sort of thing. Not me.

I was this close to getting up, saying "screw it," and taking my board home. No amount of pride was worth this kind of torture. Or so I thought.

"Charlie? Is that you?" a familiar voice asked. I closed my eyes and briefly contemplated falling back into the ocean and drowning myself.

"Natalie? What are you doing here?" Natalie Cornell had been a bully growing up. And while it was one thing to be an asshole when you're seven, it's entirely another to be one when you're approaching thirty. Now, I considered her to be my nemesis.

She stared down at me, wearing a revealing bikini that showed off her perfectly tanned skin and long legs. Well, good looks didn't count for much when you had a personality that made Hannibal Lecter seem like a nice guy.

"I come to Cos's classes twice a week. I like yoga. It keeps my body flexible and strong. What are you doing here? It can't possibly be for the same reason?"

"I'm here as part of a job. I figured, you know, why not do a casual yoga session while I'm at it? I've never done it before, but I'm sure I'll still kick your ass."

Natalie smirked down at me. "Well, step one is to actually get on the paddleboard."

"Oh, I'm down here on purpose," I lied. "I thought I'd get connected with the water first, before I head out into the bay."

"Whatever," Natalie said, rolling her eyes. "Try to get out there before the class ends."

She then climbed onto her paddleboard, on her knees, and began paddling out toward Cosmic Pegasus, who had come to a rest about a hundred yards from the shore.

I was pleased to see that despite her big talk, Natalie couldn't stand on her board, and even on her knees the board wobbled from side to side.

I narrowed my eyes. Okay, this was war. I *definitely* wasn't going to quit now.

Chapter 13

I climbed out of the water and had a look for my board. It had drifted toward the shore, the nose gently nudging the sand every few seconds in line with the tide. The paddle floated a few feet away, and I grabbed it first. Then I did the same as Natalie: I climbed onto the board on my knees, and while it tilted to the right, perilously close to dropping me right back into the ocean, I was able to shift my weight at the last second, and the board righted itself once more.

I realized then that I held the paddle with a grip strength that would make any powerlifter proud. I forced myself to relax a little bit, and I slowly brought myself up to a kneeling position. So far, so good. Dipping the paddle in the water, I pushed and headed toward Cos.

I was so intently focused on getting over there in one piece—every time a wave broke beneath me my heart leapt into my throat and a shot of adrenaline sent my heart pounding—that I didn't even notice that by the time I'd reached Cosmic Pegasus, a few other paddleboarders had joined in as well. There were maybe twelve people in total in the class, all of us in more or less a half circle around Cos, who gazed upon us with a calm expression on her face. She had dropped down to her knees as well, and was sitting on her heels, her hands pressed together in front of her chest.

Natalie was next to me, glaring openly at me, while I ignored her. I figured not giving her any attention would make her mad.

"Welcome, everyone. I hope you're all ready for an hour of peaceful practice as we say goodbye to the sun until he greets us again tomorrow," Cos began. "Let us begin by taking a deep breath and releasing the stress of the day that we all experience while living under a capitalist system. Inhale through your nose, and exhale through your mouth. Let it all go, and allow your body to reconnect with the ocean, with the earth, and with nature. Breathe in… and breathe out."

I tried to follow Cos's instructions and relax, but frankly, I was more concerned with *not* connecting with the ocean and staying on the board as it floated on the water than anything else. I silently cursed every single ad I'd ever seen of people happily cruising on paddleboards, looking like they were having a great time, laughing in the sun while they glided effortlessly across the water.

Reality was very different. At least, my reality was. Looking around at the others, some of the people in this class were obviously just as comfortable on their boards as Cos was. To my left was Natalie, but the woman on my right was busy setting up her phone on a built-in holder at the front of her board and double-checking her hair. Definitely an influencer. I was surprised she hadn't brought her boyfriend out here to swim in the water and take pictures at various angles during the session.

A couple boards over was a lady who was already *way* too into this whole yoga thing. She was in a headstand, with her feet twisted up above her in a way that made me doubt whether or not she had bones. It was both impressive and horrifying.

"And come back to center," Cos said, and I realized I'd just spent the entire time scoping out the rest of the class instead of paying attention to my breathing. Whoops. "Now, I see we've got a few new faces here today, and I'd like to welcome all of you to the practice of yoga. We're here not only to work on our bodies, but to work on our minds as well, and to find a new connection with the world as we bid farewell to the sun on its journey to the other side of the earth. With that said, let us begin this session with a simple, restorative flow that will get the blood flowing and activate the muscles we're going to use later on in this session. Let's begin with a child's pose. Come down onto your board onto all fours, then move your toes in together, move your hips back, pressing your hands into the board, and bring your forehead down as far as you can, resting it on the board if you can. If you don't have the flexibility to get there, that's completely fine. Just go as far as is comfortable. We're going to stay here for a few breaths."

Okay, as I moved into the child's pose position, I had to admit, this was actually kind of nice. I could stay here for a while. The board beneath me drifted up and down with the waves, like nature trying to rock me to sleep. Of course, I was feeling a bit of a stretch in my hip area, so it wasn't like I was drifting off, but it was nice.

"Now, from child's pose we're going to come up and move into cobra," Cos said after a minute. "Take your time, take some deep breaths, and really open up that chest."

I looked toward her and copied the movement. I glanced around at the others. Most people were in the same position as Cos. No Bones Lady at the other end, however, had her knees bent, and her legs reached so far back her feet actually touched the back of her head.

If I ever found myself in that position, someone would need to call an ambulance.

The influencer next to me had her eyes closed, a smile plastered on her face that had to be for the benefit of the camera. I didn't like cobra. It wasn't nearly as nice as child's pose. My arms were already tired from holding up my body, and I didn't feel like my chest was doing anything, let alone opening.

What did that even mean?

"Now, from here we're going to go into a high plank," Cos said. Grateful that we were switching positions, I quickly found that there was something worse than cobra pose. Much, much worse. "Use your core muscles to support your body. Squeeze those glutes, activate them."

"I'm squeezing every muscle in my body, and it's not helping," I muttered to myself as I struggled to hold the position. I'd managed it for all of around five seconds before I had to put my knees on the board, but luckily Cos didn't seem to notice.

"From here, we're going to move into a downward dog. Alternate stepping with your toes to stretch those calves, and really press into the mat with your hands. Use those shoulders, that upper body strength."

If the last few minutes had taught me anything, it was that I didn't have any upper body strength. Or lower body strength, for that matter. Or core. But hey, that hadn't stopped me yet.

I pushed against my board into a downward dog. My hamstrings and shoulders instantly started yelling at me. Well, they were just going to have to deal with it.

The class continued, and I found that this wasn't actually as bad as I thought it would be. I mean, sure, every muscle in my body was protesting what we did, but there were enough poses that didn't make me feel like someone had set my body on fire, and that gave me a bit of a break, that as the sun dipped closer and closer to the horizon I was starting to actually enjoy myself.

"You look like an elephant crossed with a baby giraffe," Natalie hissed at me from her board as we went back into downward dog toward the end of the class.

"Didn't you learn that if you can't say something

nice about someone, don't say anything at all?" I shot back. "I'd rather be ugly than a raging bitch, so I'm still way ahead of you."

Natalie snarled at me and then grabbed the paddle from the board and reached over toward me. She pressed down on my board, tipping it precariously to the left. "You think you're so clever. Well, drink a bit of seawater."

I tried to compensate for Natalie's actions by shifting my body weight to the right, but I overdid it, and the next thing I knew my board had flipped over and I was back in the water, my body shocked as it suddenly found itself submerged in the warm waters of the Pacific Ocean. Coming up for air, I spat out a mouthful of seawater and blinked the salt out of my eyes. The commotion had caused everyone else in the group to come out of their own yoga positions and stare at me.

Well, except for No Bones Lady. She was still in her downward dog, only she reached back with one hand to grab her opposite ankle. She looked ahead, completely focused on being the most flexible person on the planet.

I pulled myself back onto my board, trying to be as elegant as I could about it. But I was pretty sure I looked less like an elegant yogi who knew what they were doing and more like a lost seal trying to escape an orca.

With the most graceful grunt I could manage I finally hoisted myself back up onto the board. I looked around at the others staring at me and grinned. "I guess I took that whole 'become one with the ocean' thing too seriously."

That earned me a round of laughter from the group, and Cos looked approvingly in my direction.

"As with anything, when you practice yoga there will be times when you fall," Cos announced. "The important thing is that we get back up, as Charlie has done here."

Natalie smirked next to me. She was still obviously pleased with what she'd done. When, a few minutes later, Cos directed the class into a short round of meditation, I imagined myself pushing Natalie off her board and holding her head underwater, and I'd never felt in such a state of zen.

"Now, we end the class with an Ohm, to recenter ourselves."

After leading us through the final moments of class, Cos invited us all to enjoy our evenings, and I couldn't wait to get back to dry land. Stupid Natalie.

The sun was only just above the horizon now, the blue of the sky mixing with a rich orange, a preview of the pinks and purples that would soon create one of the incredible sunsets Maui was famous for.

I turned back to the beach and saw there was more of a crowd than when I'd come out. That was normal; incredible sunsets like these brought anyone who was nearby out to the beach to have a look. But it didn't take me long to realize this crowd wasn't looking at the sunset. They were watching someone on the beach, and my eyes landed on Rowan a moment later.

Great. How long had he been standing there? Had he seen me doing yoga? He'd had to. I was mortified.

I did my best to avoid looking at him as I paddled back to shore, sitting on my knees the entire time. Actually, it wasn't entirely on purpose that I was ignoring him. I still felt like my board was going to tip over at any second, especially as I got closer to shore and the waves began breaking.

When my feet were back on mostly solid sand, I dragged my board out of the water and felt a shape in front of me. I looked up to see Rowan's grinning face. Mine instantly went crimson. This guy was one of the biggest actors in Hollywood, he was insanely hot, and he lived in LA. Home to women with a body fat percentage in the single digits and who were as flexible as No Bones Lady over there. Neither of those things described me. I looked like a drowned bagel right now.

What made things even worse was that Natalie was still next to us.

"Hi, I'm Natalie," she purred in Rowan's direction. Instead of acknowledging her, he leaned down and whispered in my ear.

"I saw what she did out there. Want to make her jealous?"

"Absolutely," I replied.

My eyes widened as all of a sudden Rowan's lips were on mine and my breath caught in my throat. Oh my God. It had been way too long since I'd done this. What was my breath like? I thought back. I hadn't eaten any crunchy Cheetos today, right? Or munched on any raw cloves of garlic?

Those thoughts and more were swept away by Rowan's touch. His lips were soft, but his mouth commanding. His fingers grazed my skin, pressing into my hips and pulling me tight to him. I leaned into the kiss, my eyes closing automatically.

After a few seconds, he pulled away, and even though the kiss had been brief, I felt like fire coursed through every vein in my body.

I turned to Natalie, who still stood next to us. She gaped at me, her mouth opening and closing repeatedly, like a parrotfish eating algae off one of the coral reefs.

Eventually, she found her voice. "What the actual fuck?" she screeched. "You're dating Rowan McLeod?"

I grinned at her, wrapping an arm around Rowan's waist. "Rowan, meet Natalie. She's an awful human being who's not worth wasting your breath on."

"Good to know," Rowan said, moving his gaze to me and shooting me a look so loving a part of me melted, even though I knew he was just acting. "Why don't we get this board back to your car?"

He completely brushed off Natalie and picked up my board like he'd done it a million times before, taking the paddle from my other arm. He turned and walked toward the parking lot, the crowd of people watching parting like the Red Sea to make way for him.

I followed after him, but I couldn't resist. I looked back at Natalie, who still stood on the beach, looking a combination of stunned and furious.

I grinned and flashed her a finger wave and a wink before turning back to Rowan.

"Thank you for that," I said to him quietly, trying not to be overheard. People were taking selfies with Rowan as he walked past, while others simply stared wide-eyed. A couple even stopped him to take a photo with him, and he took a few smiling pictures before asking the crowd for a bit of privacy. A couple of especially enthusiastic fans followed us to the parking lot, but another couple of pictures later and the two of us were by ourselves.

"This one's me," I said, motioning to Queenie.

"Great. I hope I didn't cross a line. But I was watching you out there on the water, and I saw that woman flip you over. I figured the two of you weren't friends."

I laughed dryly. "You can say that again. She's been my nemesis since we were seven. She was bullying a girl who would eventually become my best friend, so I made her eat a sand sandwich."

Rowan laughed. "I wouldn't expect anything else. I assume you were here looking into Crystal's death?"

"Is it that obvious that I'm not a regular at yoga class?" I asked with a chuckle.

"Well, I wasn't going to put it that way," Rowan replied as he deftly pressed on the valve and twisted it, releasing the air from my paddleboard on the ground. "I think it's cool that you did it, especially if it was outside your comfort zone."

"It definitely was. But yeah, I was looking into Crystal's death. I wanted to get a read on Cos."

"And what do you think?"

I shrugged. "She doesn't seem to have a motive."

"I don't know her well. I only spoke to her briefly that night at the restaurant. But she seems to genuinely believe in all that hippie stuff. I would be surprised if she was a killer. She seems to be much more the forgive-and-forget type."

"You'd be surprised at what kinds of people kill others," I said wryly. "I know I've gotten a shock a couple of times. And frankly, a part of me feels like I've died a little bit after that yoga session, and it's all Cos's fault."

Rowan laughed. "Which part?"

"My legs. And my arms. And my core. I wish I had a six-pack. Yoga would be so much easier."

"Well, I can't argue with that logic."

"Listen, thanks for helping me out before. With Natalie. She's really spent her whole life trying to bully me, and nothing feels better than being able to throw it right back into her face."

"Anytime," Rowan said with a smile as he deftly rolled the paddleboard back up and hoisted it into the carry bag.

"This isn't your first time using one of these things, is it?"

"Nope. I love paddleboarding. It's a nice way to relax. I have one back in LA."

"I don't think I gave you credit before for how good an actor you are. If I didn't know any better, I would have said you were actually into that kiss."

Rowan paused what he was doing and looked at me, a mischievous glint in his eye. "Who says I was acting?"

A stupid smile spread across my face as the back of my neck flushed with heat. "Oh, come on. Don't be ridiculous."

"You're the one being ridiculous if you think I wouldn't want to kiss you."

Okay, this conversation was veering way too close to places I wasn't super comfortable with, so I quickly changed the subject. "Can I give you a ride back to the hotel?"

"Sure," Rowan replied, seemingly unfazed by complete one-eighty of topic. "Thanks."

"What were you doing on the beach tonight, anyway?"

"What everyone else was doing: enjoying the sunset. I come out most nights around this time and take a stroll along the path that wanders through Wailea. After it gets dark, I tend not to be recognized, especially if I'm wearing a hat, so it's nice to be able to go out and have a bit of a break from life."

"I can imagine," I said as I hopped into the driver's seat of the car. Rowan hoisted the bag with the paddle-board into the back and joined me on the passenger side. "Everyone always says they want to be famous, but it really becomes your whole life, doesn't it?"

"It does. You saw the people on the beach today, and at the bar last night. That's actually not even that bad. I've gone to cities where I've been swarmed by thousands of people. They have to close down stores for me if I want to go shopping. And it's all day, every day. Now, don't get me wrong, I'm grateful for the life I live, and I really enjoy meeting my fans most of the time. But it's also difficult when your job overwhelms your entire life. So sometimes, I like to go out and be anonymous for once, and it's easier after the sun has gone down."

"I can understand that, actually. It's been strange just seeing my picture on TMZ. I can't imagine living my life like that all the time."

"It's not the easiest, but I knew going into it that this is how it would be. I think the important thing is to stay grounded. Ultimately, I have to know who I am, not who the papers report me to be. I can't care about what they say, I can't care about what the general public thinks. If you let it get to your head, then it changes you. I don't want to let that change me."

"No. I think that's smart. People don't normally think about that aspect of the job. That it really is a life."

"It really is. But then, every job has its challenges and its opportunities, I suppose. This way, I get to make incredible movies, which has been my dream since I was a kid, and I get to live a life I couldn't have dreamed of growing up in Vancouver."

"Right, I knew you're from Canada."

"I practically grew up on the hills of Grouse Mountain. But don't worry, I also ate my fair share of maple syrup."

"I would hope so," I said with a chuckle. "Nothing like fitting the stereotype."

"Well, my parents were ski bums and not maple farmers, but close enough."

I pulled into the front of the Maui Diamond

Resort. "Thanks again for everything. Whether or not you meant the kiss."

"I definitely meant it," Rowan said with a wink as he got out of the car and headed into the lobby.

I wasn't used to this. Rowan wasn't like the men I normally dated. I mean, like three years ago I dated a guy who thought "I came, I saw, I conquered" was an original quote by Jay-Z. I had notoriously awful taste in men, but Rowan was different. He was ultra-famous, sure. But he was good-looking, kind, quick on his feet, and down-to-earth. Plus, he was totally willing to piss off Natalie Cornell for me, which automatically rocketed him up the ranks in my books.

I shook my head. We weren't dating, anyway. It was just one kiss. Why was I such a mess when it came to my personal life?

I pulled back out onto the road and drove to Dot's apartment. I couldn't think about Rowan anymore; I had a missing guy to hunt down.

Chapter 14

Rosie answered the door when I arrived, and pulled it open to let me in. "Dot tells me you've got yourself a new case. A missing person."

"Right. A lawyer named John Waters. He sounds like a peach. Lied to his wife about getting laid off from his job."

"Well, unfortunately for us, he's not active on any social media sites," Dot announced from her spot at the computer. "I've spent half the afternoon scouring the web for his digital footprint, and let me tell you, there's not much of one."

"Have you been in the ocean?" Rosie asked as I went over to the computer, her eyebrows rising slightly.

"I don't want to talk about it," I muttered, and Dot grinned.

"Never mess with the water. Anyway, speaking of messing with, I don't know what's happened to John Waters, but it's probably not good."

"All right, what do you have?" I pulled a chair up and sat down, leaning forward to get a good look at the screen.

"First, you tell us about the dinner with Rowan," Dot said.

I shrugged. "It was fine. I don't think he did it. He hasn't got anything remotely resembling a motive."

"That you know of," Rosie warned. "But how was he as a person?"

"Very nice. Kind," I said, heat rising up the back of my neck.

"You're blushing!" Dot said accusingly.

I feigned ignorance. "Am I?"

"You totally are. Spill. What happened?"

I recounted the entire story, from dinner last night to the kiss after paddleboarding today. When I was finished, Dot squealed with excitement. "Our little Charlie's growing up."

"I am not," I shot back, certain that my face was the color of an overripe tomato.

"It's a good thing, Charlie. You're allowed to have some fun," Rosie said. "Although personally, I'd recommend sticking to people who aren't murder suspects. Still, I agree with you, it seems unlikely that he's the culprit."

"Well, now that I've told you two everything, what do you have on our missing person?" I asked, trying to turn the attention away from me.

"John Waters. Fifty-two years old. Born in Minneapolis, Minnesota. Moved to Maui when he was seven. Did his undergrad and law school at UH," Dot announced.

"I can see why his parents moved here," Rosie muttered. "I spent a weekend in Minnesota in January once and let me tell you, it makes Moscow look like a tropical paradise."

"Coming out of law school he tried to start his own firm, but shut that down after two years and took the job he had up until six months ago. Married his wife Vanessa when he was twenty, and they had a daughter a year later. Has a house Upcountry near Kula worth about two million. Frankly, this guy was just hitting all the squares in *The Game of Life*. All he had left to do was retire, break a hip, go to the hospital, catch pneumonia, and die."

"Well, there's a happy thought."

"Might be better than what actually happened to him."

"Which is?"

"Don't have a clue. What I can tell you is that since yesterday morning, he hasn't used his credit or debit cards or made any phone calls. However, his car's GPS tracker still appears to be active. So, if you'd like to check it out in the morning, we can see what his car is doing at Haleakala National Park."

I raised my eyebrows. "Maybe he decided to enjoy the sunset? Can you tell how long the car has been there?"

Dot shook her head. "Nope. The tracker in his car doesn't show the history. At least, not in the database I was able to get into."

Rosie glanced at the clock. "Well, if we want to get in before reservations are necessary, we'd better go now. Or, we could wait until after seven o'clock tomorrow."

Due to the popularity of watching the sunrise from the summit of Haleakala, reservations were required between the hours of three and seven a.m., and they sold out fast enough that there was no chance we were getting a last-minute spot.

"You know what sounds like a terrible idea? Driving up to the summit of the mountain now, getting there at midnight, and then trying to find a lost guy who may or may not be near his car in pitch black, at the end of winter, with the wind howling at a hundred miles an hour," I said. "One of us is likely to go missing, too, if we do that."

"Speak for yourself," Rosie said. "You think *that's* hard? I've had to cross-country ski across two valleys in the Caucasus Mountains while a couple of French snipers hid in the trees trying to pick me off."

"Okay, so Rosie would be fine."

"And so would I," Dot said, in a tone that said she would accept no argument to the contrary.

"Got it. In that case, *I* don't want to get blown off the top of the mountain and die alone in a field of sharp lava stones. But that said, his wife is a client, and I am worried. So, as much as I hate this idea, I think we should see if he's at least with his car. Which means heading up there now."

"We will need to bundle up," Rosie said. "Charlie was complaining about the weather up there, but she's right. It's March, and the wind is cutting. Dot, do you have enough winter clothes for all of us?"

"Sure do. But that said, we live on Maui. It's not like I have to break this stuff out on a weekly basis, so it might be a bit dated."

"That's fine," I replied. "As long as I'm warm, I don't care what I'm wearing."

Truly spoken like someone who hadn't seen Dot's closet.

Ten minutes later, we were ready to go. When Dot said her winter clothing options were dated, she was not kidding. I looked like a cool teenager in an ad for The Gap. If it was 1993, anyway. The jacket that best fit me—and looked warmest—was an insulated coat with a chevron pattern along the front. The bottom part was white with black zebra stripes. Above it were chevrons in neon pink and bright lilac. The top of the jacket was a turquoise so bright the ocean would be jealous of it. Inside, the lining was the same zebra print. I was pretty sure I'd owned this exact same jacket when I was five.

Rosie wore a retro Detroit Red Wings jacket in red and white, with the team logo on the front and one armband. The other had the NHL's Western Conference logo. It was at least three sizes too big for her, and reached halfway down her thighs,

Dot, on the other hand, looked like a unicorn vomited all over her jacket. It featured at least five different shades of pinks and purples, in rainbow-like stripes along the front. She strutted around proudly, and I had to admit, she wore it well.

"We should take Rosie's CR-V," I suggested. "It'll be nice and warm in there."

"For someone so young, you really don't have much of a sense of adventure, do you?"

"No, I just know how cold it's going to be at the top. It's going to be in the thirties, with a wind that's going to make it feel like the tens. I didn't leave Seattle so I could know what real winter in early March feels like."

"You left Seattle so you didn't get chopped up and fed to the fishes in Puget Sound," Dot pointed out. "But fine. You can bring a blanket, if you're going to be a baby about it."

"I am, thank you very much," I replied. The three of us headed down to the car, and I had a queen-sized Sherpa blanket with me. It was altogether too hot while we were still down in Kihei—the lows still generally didn't drop below the mid-sixties, even at night—but I knew once we drove ten thousand feet higher, I was going to need it.

Rosie drove, and Dot took the passenger seat, leaving me to spread out with my blanket in the back. We started off with the air conditioner going, heading north to Kahului before turning south once more—they really needed to build that highway to Upcountry—and beginning the slow, steady rise to the top of the crater.

This road featured about two hundred switchbacks—well, it felt that way, anyway—and while I was fully confident in Rosie's driving, I still wasn't entirely comfortable being so close to the edge of the road that simply dropped away. I assumed on the other side was a hundreds-of-feet drop that would send us plunging to our deaths. The fact that I couldn't actually *see* over the edge wasn't especially helpful in negating this fear.

After about an hour, we reached the main visitor's center as well as the gate to pay our entrance fee into the national park. Rosie paid the fee and continued driving, while I kept my eyes peeled for Nene, the state bird of Hawaii. Unfortunately, since it was now very much past sunset and the Hawaiian goose was diurnal, I figured my odds of seeing one were pretty low. Still, it wasn't like I had anything else to do.

"Up here," Dot said eventually. Directly in front of us was a single-story building and a parking lot designed to fit about a hundred cars. Dim lights shone from the building, and a sign indicated the way to the bathrooms. Only a handful of cars remained in the lot. Rosie drove along until the headlights illuminated a late-model C-class Mercedes.

"That's the one," Dot said. Rosie pulled up next to it and killed the engine. We got out of the car, and even though I was expecting the temperature to be colder, I still shivered involuntarily.

It was cold, sure, but to make matters worse, the wind was absolutely howling. My blanket whipped around me, despite the fact that we were partially protected by the building and the mound of lava that led to the true summit about half a mile further along the road.

I couldn't imagine being up there and exposed in this kind of weather.

Still, I had a job to do, and I couldn't go back to Vanessa and explain to her that I didn't know what happened to her husband because it was a bit chilly.

I pressed my face against the glass off the driver's side door and peered inside, but it was quickly obvious that the car was empty, and when I pulled on the handle, it was locked. "Well, he's not here," I said.

"I've been meaning to look into how to create duplicate keys for cars controlled by electronics," Dot said. "It's too bad I haven't done it yet. We could have gotten into his car that way."

"What about tracking his phone?" I asked. "Could it be done around here?"

"He hasn't used his phone since he went missing. We could always triangulate and see where it last pinged against cell towers, but it won't give us an accurate location. Especially not up here, where we're not close to a cluster of cell towers."

I frowned. "Okay. So we have to assume that John came up here himself. But why?"

"There are a number of hiking trails along here," Rosie suggested with a shrug. "Could it be possible he came up to do, say, Sliding Sands Trail, and got lost?"

"It could be," I said, looking around. "There's no park rangers near here, are there? Vanessa didn't mention him being an avid hiker, but you never know."

The three of us scoured the area near the car a little bit more, but there was nothing to be seen. The interior was neat and tidy, but there was no sign of John.

I took in the surroundings, wrapping my blanket

around me more tightly, and it wasn't entirely because of the cold weather. I had a bad feeling about this. There was nowhere to go from here that didn't lead to death by exposure. John obviously wasn't in the visitor's center. It was closed for the night. Apart from that, the only buildings near here were the observatories at the summit, but they were locked and for scientist use only. He certainly didn't qualify.

"I'm going to check the bathrooms, just in case," I said, not expecting much. Park rangers patrolled here every day, and at this point, John had been missing for almost forty-eight hours. If he'd spent most of that time here, and if he was in trouble, he would have been seen by now. In fact, I expected that by morning the rangers would probably put an alert out given as his car was still in the lot, if they hadn't already.

"Good idea," Rosie said approvingly. "I'll have a look around the building. Dot, do a scan of the fields nearby. We meet back here in a few minutes."

The three of us separated, looking for John, in case he was near his car somewhere. I entered the bathrooms and checked the men's room, but it was completely abandoned. There wasn't a soul to be seen. I looked in the women's as well, just in case, but no. Then, just to be sure, I checked the rest of the building that was still accessible, but there was no sign of the man.

I returned to Rosie's car, and a few minutes later the other two returned. From the looks on their faces, I already knew before they told me that they'd seen no sign of John.

"Well, I won't pretend it's a good thing," Rosie said, her expression grim. "There are experienced hikers who do overnight trips in this region, but they're few and far between."

"And none of us heard anything about John that might indicate he was an avid hiker," Dot said. "What was he doing up here?"

I shrugged. "Escaping the fact that he goes home every night and lies to his wife about having a job?"

"Maybe," Dot said, pressing her lips together. "Still, I don't like it. You don't need to be a hiking fanatic to know that this is a dangerous place to get lost on a hike. It's long, it's desolate, and the altitude will get you."

"I've done Sliding Sands quite a few times," Rosie said as she pulled out from the parking spot. "It's miles long, and it's downhill right from the start. If you go too far, it's very dangerous. Climbing back up isn't easy at the best of times, let alone up here where the air is so thin."

Just as we were leaving, a white truck passed us, adorned with the dark-green stripes of the National Park Service. Rosie turned the car around and flashed her high beams at him a couple times, and the driver of the truck parked in the lot and got out of his truck.

It was hard to make out details of the driver's features from inside the car, with only the headlights shining onto him, but the man was dressed in the standard national park khakis, with a jacket on top. He was about six foot two, Hawaiian, with deep-set eyes and a strong chin. His smile was friendly as he came out to greet us.

"What can I do for you ladies tonight?" he asked as the three of us got out of the car. To his credit, he didn't blink an eye at the three of us who looked like we'd hopped right out of a jock jams music video. "Did you see tonight's sunset?"

"Not tonight," Rosie replied. "In fact, we're looking for someone."

"Have you seen this man?" Dot asked, pulling up a photo of John Waters on her phone and holding it out to the ranger.

"Him? Oh, yeah, I have actually. That's his car over there. The white Mercedes. Saw him yesterday morning. He told me he was doing an overnight trip, and not to worry about the car still being in the lot tonight. Not everyone thinks to let the rangers know, but I reported it, so that way no alarm bells will go off."

I raised my eyebrows. "Did he seem to know what he was doing? Have an overnight pack with him?"

The man shrugged. "I'm not sure. He had just gotten out of his car when he found me. I have to imagine he did. Who does an overnight hike with just a bottle of water? Why? Has something happened to him?"

"I'm a private investigator. His wife has reported him missing," I said.

The man frowned. "Why didn't he tell her he was going on a hike? Did they have a fight?"

"No. It's a long story, but basically, I think there's something weird going on here, and that you should put an alert out on this guy. I don't know how you do it in the park."

"Sure. I can do that. You think he might be out there injured somewhere?"

"Or worse. But unless his wife is lying to me, and I don't think she is, she has absolutely no idea where he's gone."

The man turned to Dot. "Any chance you can airdrop me that photo? I'd like to have it so I can pass it around to the other rangers, and anyone who might be going where he did."

"Sure," Dot said, tapping away at the phone for a minute. The ranger took down our information and thanked us, and we were soon back on our way down the mountain. Even though we'd only been outside for twenty minutes, tops, and wearing actual jackets, I was still a little bit on the colder side, and while Rosie and Dot didn't complain about the cold, Rosie had cranked the heat up as high as it would go.

"So, I'm just going to say it: John Waters is dead, isn't he?" I finally said after about five minutes.

"Yeah, he's real dead," Dot replied. "If he came up here to hike yesterday morning and hasn't come back to his car yet, after pretending to his wife that he was just going to work, then he's a goner."

"I don't know," Rosie mused. "We have a lot of questions that haven't been answered yet."

"Like what?" Dot asked.

"For one thing, what was he doing hiking here when he told his wife he was going to work? Why did he tell the park ranger he was going to be hiking overnight if he intended to be back home after standard work hours?"

The car delved into silence. Rosie was right. It was easy to say John Waters had just gotten lost on a hike and died, but that was an important question, and one that didn't appear to have an easy answer.

"Well, if he is out there, then the question becomes this: is he alive, or is he dead?" I said. "If he actually *did* come expecting to hike, he should hopefully have been prepared for the conditions. I don't think he could have spent forty-eight hours up here with no protective gear, food, or water, but if for some reason he did come to spend a few days up here without telling his wife, I suppose there's no reason to assume the worst. But then we always get back to Rosie's question: why not tell Vanessa that he wasn't going to come home for a couple of days?"

"There's something fishy going on here," Rosie said. "We don't have the full story. We're missing something. Dot, are you sure you don't know anything else about this guy?"

Dot shrugged. "I'll see what I can dig up when we get back home. When I saw the car was here, I kind of figured he'd be near it. And besides, you never know. Now that the park rangers know about it, there's a good chance they'll find him in the next day or so. Alive or dead."

"I'm personally hoping for alive," I said. "But I don't know. Maybe he just wanted to die and didn't want his wife to worry. Something like that."

"Possibly. Are you working tomorrow?"

I shook my head. "No. But I have to get in touch with Bill Jamieson. I'll ask Marion for help with that. I want to talk to her about her ex-husband, anyway. I can come by either before or after I do that."

"Make it after. That way, I'll hopefully have found some more information about John that might let us know what he was up to. Or, alternately, it will have given the rangers enough time to find his body."

"There's no guarantee they will if he's lost up there," Rosie pointed out. "Sliding Sands Trail is extremely desolate. There are a million places one could get lost, and they're not all easily accessible. He could also have fallen off the trail, rolled behind a pile of rock, and we'd never know. His body could easily be lost forever."

"I hope not. Vanessa seemed nice, and I'd like her to get some closure. So far, I'm not getting great vibes from what I know about John, though."

"You never know. It sounds as though he was going through some rough times," Rosie said quietly. "I saw it a lot at the bank. In the early eighties, especially. The Iranian revolution, the energy crisis in seventy-nine, it all added up to some difficult times for people back then. There were customers I saw every day who struggled, and it changed how they acted quite significantly."

"Still, losing your job and not telling your spouse about it for months, pretending to go to work every day?" I said, shaking my head. "That's ridiculous and stupid and toxic, no matter how you look at it."

"I do agree with you there. Marriages should be based on mutual trust and communication, and lying to your spouse about your employment status for months on end is just… the opposite of that. But I'm speaking about his actions over the last day or so."

"Well, hopefully Dot and her magical computer can dig up some answers for us."

"It's not the computer that's magical, it's my skills on it," Dot shot at me from the passenger seat.

"Noted."

Chapter 15

Once the three of us returned to Kihei I gave Dot back her jacket and drove home. Zoe was sitting on the couch, curled up with Coco while reading a science fiction book. When I entered, she put the book down.

"Any news on the killer?"

I shook my head. "No. Although I saw Natalie Cornell today."

Zoe made a face. "Better you than me."

"We were in the same stand-up paddleboarding class. She knocked me off my board into the water when everyone was doing downward dog so no one would see her do it."

"It's good to know she's just as immature as ever."

"Anyway, Rowan McLeod was watching from the beach, and when we came in, he kissed me."

Zoe's mouth dropped open. "What?"

"Yeah. It was a surprise, and I don't know how I

feel about it. I thought he was just doing it to make Natalie jealous, but then he told me afterwards it wasn't entirely acting, and I don't know what's going on."

"Let me guess: in order to hide the fact that you felt super awkward about it, you decided to just make a snarky comment and change the subject quickly instead of having to deal with the possibility of talking about feelings with somebody, especially a man."

"Well, when you put it that way, it sounds like a bad idea."

"Ya think?" Zoe said with a smile. "Did it scare him off?"

"No."

"Well, that's something. What do you think of him?"

"I don't know," I said. "He's nice. I like him. I like spending time with him. That's not the problem."

"So what is the problem?" Zoe asked.

I shrugged. "I don't know."

"Is the problem possibly that you've found someone who's kind, stable, and could potentially be a fun fling or a longer-term romantic partner and you're terrified of it going well, and trying to come up with ways to sabotage it?"

"I swear, whoever convinced you to go into emergency medicine instead of psychology did the world a disservice. And no, I'm not sabotaging this because I'm scared. It wouldn't be a long-term thing anyway. Rowan lives in LA."

A small smile crept up into the corner of Zoe's

mouth. "And you've decided you want to live here on Maui long term."

"I guess I do, yeah. I like it here. And I'm starting a career of my own."

"Okay. So long term is out. That's fine. What about short term? Nothing stopping you having a fling. After all, I heard one of our neighbors did the same a few decades ago." Zoe shot me a wink.

"I am *not* Vesper."

"Oh please, she's like looking at you twenty-five years in the future."

"I fully intend to have both my legs by the time I'm her age."

"I certainly hope you do. Anyway, I know what you're doing. You're changing the subject, yet again."

"I am not. You're the one who started talking about my career."

"I really wasn't. Anyway, I think if you like Rowan and you want to have a fling with him, and he's also into it, there's nothing wrong with that."

"Yeah. I don't know. I just… I don't know if I want to."

"Okay. Then it doesn't have to go anywhere."

"I just don't know *why* it feels weird. Like, there's nothing wrong with him. No glaring red flags, no talk of crazy ex-girlfriends, nothing. So why am I hesitating?"

Zoe shrugged. "Sometimes, someone just isn't right for you. And even if they are, it might not be the right time. You can't know. But trust your instincts. They're there for a reason. If you're not into having a relationship with him, then there's nothing wrong with that, even if there isn't anything wrong with him."

I sighed and dug through the fridge until I found half a leftover sub from the other day. I unwrapped it and started munching down on it. I was starving.

"Anyway, Natalie was super pissed," I said with a grin. "So that worked out really well. I wish you could have seen it. She couldn't *believe* Rowan McLeod kissed me. And he totally brushed her off when she tried to introduce herself to him."

Zoe laughed. "I bet. Well, as much as I'd like to be a bigger person and say that school was a long time ago, I feel like this is just karma catching up to her."

"Exactly. And it's so much sweeter when you get to see it happen."

"How was stand-up paddleboarding, anyway?"

"Hard. It wasn't so much stand-up paddleboarding as wobbling-on-my-knees paddleboarding."

"That's how I felt my first time too. Don't worry, it gets easier."

"I don't intend to ever find out."

Zoe snorted. "Oh, come on. It's a lot of fun. It's a great workout, and you get to be on the water."

"I'm interested in zero of those things."

"Spoken like somebody who has never gone paddleboarding in the morning and been met by a curious pod of dolphins."

"I saw a meme once that said dolphins attack people."

"Oh, well, if you saw it on the internet, it must be true. That's why everyone knows dolphins are notorious killers and everyone hates them. Besides, you cannot live on a subtropical island in the middle of the Pacific Ocean and not like dolphins. That's just not allowed."

"You're the only person on the planet that would make the distinction between tropical and subtropical. Anyway, I can't paddleboard. I can't even stand up on the board."

"That's fine. You kneel until you work toward it. You've driven along the highway to the west coast. You've seen the hundreds of people paddleboarding there in the mornings. They all started from nothing, too. Come on, I'll take you out one morning, and I promise I won't knock you into the water. We'll have fun."

"Are you going to talk about how we're connected to the water, and how we're bidding hello to the sun, and what kind of crystals we're wearing?"

Zoe laughed. "Only if you're into that."

"Well, not really. Though I have to admit, Cos was really nice about the fact that I showed up to her class and didn't have a clue what I was doing."

"That's good. I can't stand people who make beginners feel inferior. We were all beginners once, at everything. There's no shame in it. Being bad at something is the only way we can eventually become good."

"As much as I agree with that sentiment, I have no intention of ever becoming good at paddleboarding."

"All right, all right. I won't bug you about it again. Not until tomorrow, anyway. Whose board did you use?"

"Leslie's. I'm going to take it back to her place in

the morning. She told me I could use it for longer if I wanted to, but nah."

Zoe laughed. "Well, you tried. It doesn't sound like you think Cos is the killer."

I shook my head. "No. I don't. At least, I don't think so. She didn't appear to have a motive. And honestly, she's too much of a hippie."

"She's not putting the whole thing on to drum up more business?"

"Her name is Cosmic Pegasus. If she's faking it, she's pretty devoted to the grift."

"That's a good point. Especially since she's had the name for longer than someone's been trying to kill your client."

"I need to call Marion. I want to organize a meeting with her ex-husband, but I don't know how to do that, because unlike Jake, I don't have a badge that can get me in to see basically anyone," I grumbled. "And he wouldn't let me join his interview."

"I can't entirely blame him on that point."

"I can. He could have just told Bill I was a cop too. There's no law against that."

"There absolutely *is* a law against that," Zoe said, her expression changing to one of amusement.

"Yeah, but it's not one of those laws anyone cares about unless you're doing something bad. And I'm not. I'm trying to find a killer."

"Sure. But Jake still isn't going to bend the law for you, just because you think it's a law that shouldn't apply."

"I know. I tried. Anyway, hopefully Marion will help me."

"Well, it's in her best interest to do so, if the killer is coming after her. What do you know about her husband?"

"Not much, to be honest. Let me give her a call, and then I'm going to see what I can find about him."

"Sounds good."

I went into the bedroom and left Zoe to her book while I dialed Marion's number. I called the direct line she had given me, and she answered on the second ring.

"Charlie," she greeted me warmly. "How is your investigation going?"

"I have a few leads I'm following up on. Listen, I'm wondering if you could help me get in touch with your ex-husband."

"Bill? What does he have to do with any of this?"

"He was seen at the bar the night Crystal was killed."

Marion inhaled sharply on the other end of the line. "Bill? Are you sure?"

"One hundred percent. Did you know he was on the island?"

"No. I didn't have a clue. As you can imagine, the two of us don't exactly keep each other appraised of our whereabouts."

"Of course."

"Okay. If you need to speak with him, I can make that happen. Listen, do you mind coming down to see me tomorrow morning? I want to discuss this case with you a little bit further."

"Sure. That's no problem. Where do you want to meet?"

"Can you come to my room? Suite 902 at the Maui Diamond. Tomorrow at nine. Stop by the front desk for a key to let you up to the penthouse."

"I'll see you there."

"Thank you, Charlie."

I hung up the phone, biting my lip. I wished I had more information for Marion. I wished I knew who wanted her dead, for one. Right now all I had were the barest threads of leads. Aaron Lewis was still at the top of my list of suspects, but I needed to speak with Bill Jamieson as well before I ruled him out.

I went back to the living room and grabbed my laptop. Zoe had put her book away and was now scrolling on her phone. "Your kiss with Rowan made the gossip sites again," she said with a grin.

I groaned. "You're kidding."

"Nope. Front and center on TMZ. You're also on E! Online's top photos for today, and there's even been a Buzzfeed article written about you."

"How? Who was taking pictures? Okay, I know it was one of the dozens of people on the beach watching us, but *come on*. I don't want my picture everywhere. I bet I look ridiculous too."

"Actually, it's pretty great," Zoe said with a grin.

I opened a new browser window and went to the E! Online website. Sure enough, as soon as the page loaded, I was met with a picture of me wrapped up in Rowan's arms. I was pleased to see that not a lot of me was visible, my body enveloped in his. And my ass looked great in the bathing suit. This was a definite upgrade over the last picture of me that had been plastered all over the gossip pages.

Even better, however, was the shot of Natalie standing behind us. She was close enough to still be in focus in the shot. Her brow was furrowed in anger, and her mouth was open, teeth visible, as if she was about to yell at us. Her hands were in front of her, held up like she didn't know what was going on.

It was absolutely perfect.

I cackled. "Okay, I take it back. I hope everybody in the world sees this photo. She looks so angry."

"The Buzzfeed article says this is going to be the new distracted boyfriend meme template," Zoe said, chuckling. "I don't like to wish ill on Natalie, but I can't help but laugh at this."

"I'm not nearly as good a person as you, so I totally wish her ill, and this is hilarious. She looks like someone just took a dump in her coffee."

Zoe snorted. "You really have a way with words."

"I'm not wrong, though."

"No, you're not. She isn't going to be happy when she sees that photo."

"She's probably already seen it," I said with a grin. "And just in case she hasn't, I'm going to send it to her. I wish we could have been there when she saw it. Anyway, I guess I should stop gloating about this and actually look up Bill Jamieson."

"That's a good idea. Are you seeing him tomorrow?"

"Yeah. Marion's going to organize it."

"Good."

I tapped away at the computer, still feeling a bit of a high from having seen that photo. Not only did I look significantly better than I did in the photo with Marion —even though it wasn't really possible to make out who I was—but Natalie couldn't have looked more angry.

Still, this wasn't my focus right now. I looked up everything I could about Bill Jamieson.

"Okay, so I can't see anything that would explain why he's on Maui right now," I said to Zoe after about ten minutes of searching. "There's no information out there about a movie he might be producing."

"He could be here on vacation," Zoe offered.

"Yeah. I guess that's most likely. Although, if you were a rich old dude who could afford to go literally anywhere in the world, would you really take your vacation on the same tiny little island as your ex-wife, who's been here for a month and has been pictured here regularly? It's not like he can pretend he didn't know she was there."

"That's a good point," Zoe admitted. "Still, maybe that was the point. Maybe he just wanted her to see him. Make her jealous, or whatever. We don't know the dynamics of their relationship."

"No, that's true. That's why I want to speak to him. And to her too. I want to know what the real story is, the one that didn't necessarily make the papers."

"Yeah."

"There are a lot of articles out there about their divorce, though. It wasn't pretty. And of course, because this is the way the world works, it seems to have affected her life negatively more than his."

Zoe rolled her eyes. "Of course it has."

"In fact, from an outsider's perspective, Bill Jamieson definitely would be called the winner of the divorce. He started dating his personal trainer a few months after the papers were signed. He's produced two blockbusters in the past year, and he even won an Oscar. Meanwhile, Marion's last few movies have been flops. She also hasn't been romantically linked with anyone. There was one article which suggested she might be having a fling with Aaron, so I wonder if that might have something to do with why she dropped him as her yoga teacher."

"It's possible," Zoe said slowly. "It makes me think more of her that she didn't immediately start dating the first thing with a pulse within arm's reach."

"That's a good point. She's always had a bit of this ethereal aura about her. Like she's better than the rest of us. More elegant. More poised. More perfect. And I think if she'd gotten divorced and immediately started going out with someone who wasn't worthy, it would have reflected badly on her. But then, what do I know? We're still just gossiping about people whose lives are lived out on tabloid pages."

"Right. Without getting information from the source, we don't know what's going on. For example, the Buzzfeed article I saw about you kissing Rowan didn't even identify you. They called you a "mystery woman" who had captured his heart, and one source reported that you were an actress playing a minor character in the movie he was filming."

I snorted. "They couldn't have been more wrong."

"Exactly. You'll get more information tomorrow when you speak to Marion. Get your information from the source. That's my advice."

"You're right. You're always right. I should run all my decisions past you before I do anything in life."

Zoe laughed. "I'm always only a text message away. But life wouldn't be nearly as interesting if you didn't do your own thing."

"Well, as long as my train wreck of a life is entertaining to you, I guess that's something."

Before Zoe had a chance to reply, my phone rang. It was my mom.

"Thank you for calling the Roadkill Café, you kill it we grill it. How can I help you?"

"I know it's you, Charlie," my mom answered, obviously not impressed.

"Mom! Have you heard about my new restaurant? It's my latest business venture."

"No, but I have seen the picture of you with your new boyfriend. Why didn't you tell me you were dating Rowan McLeod?"

I closed my eyes. Of *course* my mom had already seen the picture. It had been on the internet for all of ten minutes.

"How do you even know that's me? You can't see my face."

"For one thing, Natalie Cornell wouldn't look nearly as upset if it were someone else."

"Haha, yeah, that's totally true," I said with a grin.

"And secondly, you're my daughter. I gave birth to that butt; I recognize it in photos."

"Cool, so that's how we're phrasing that, is it?"

"Charlie! How could you date Rowan and not tell me?"

"Because I'm not dating Rowan? There's always that."

"I wasn't born yesterday, dear. A man doesn't kiss a woman like that if there's not something going on between them. You don't have to call it dating. I know with your generation, you don't like labels. But whatever's going on with you, I can't believe you didn't tell your mother."

"Really? You can't believe it? You can't see a single reason why if there *was* something going on you'd be the last person I would tell?"

"No, of course not. Now, tell me everything. In fact, you know what? He can tell me himself. Why don't the two of you come over to my place for dinner on Sunday? I know I'm not really set up to host one of the biggest superstars in Hollywood, but I'll have it catered."

"That's not happening, Mom. There's nothing happening between us. Rowan kissed me to make Natalie jealous. That's all."

"No man kisses a woman like that if he's not into her. I can tell from that photo. Now, don't you dare tell me that man is into you and you're too focused on whatever it is that goes on in that head of yours to notice."

"I'm coming up to a tunnel Mom, I'm going to lose reception."

"There is one tunnel on this island and it's like a hundred feet long."

"You're breaking up. I'll talk to you later," I said, making terrible static noises into the phone before mashing the end call button.

Zoe had been stifling back laughter which she finally released when I hung up the phone.

"I only heard one side of the conversation, and it's all I needed to hear. Good to see Carmen hasn't changed a bit. I assume she's picking out names for her new, famous grandbaby?"

"I should warn Rowan he's going to need a restraining order," I muttered. "Actually, come to think of it, I probably will too."

Chapter 16

The next morning, I drove Queenie to the Maui Diamond Resort. I stopped by the front desk to get a key that would give me access to the ninth floor, and after showing ID and checking it against the list of authorized people, I stepped into the elevator and went up to the ninth floor, where Marion's penthouse suite was located. I found it quickly and knocked on the door.

Instead of Marion answering, there came a shout from inside the suite. Before I had a chance to decide what I was going to do, the door swung open. In front of me was a figure wearing a black mask over his face. He was taller than me, and that was the last thought I had before he raised his hand and everything went black.

My eyes fluttered open, trying to adjust to the light. My head was pounding, and a ringing sound coursed through my ears.

"Charlie? Charlie, are you awake?"

I blinked multiple times, trying to bring the world into focus. I was lying on the floor somewhere, a pillow behind my head. Beneath me, cool tiles pressed against my skin. In front of me was a floor-to-ceiling window offering a view onto the blue sky above. A face popped into view. It was Marion. There was a cut above her eyebrow, and a bruise was forming on her neck.

"What happened?" I finally managed to croak out. "Are you okay?"

"I'm fine. How are you feeling? You got hit on the head pretty hard."

I tried to sit up, but my head began to spin, so I gave up on that idea pretty quickly and leaned back down on the pillow. "I'm okay. My head hurts. What happened? Who was that?"

"An intruder," Marion said quietly. "He was here to kill me. He would have succeeded, too, if you hadn't arrived when you did. You saved my life."

At Marion's words, bile rose into my mouth. "I need to know what happened."

"No, you need to relax. Amber is coming back with drinks. She was out getting my coffee when it happened."

"Have you called the police?"

"Not yet. I… I'm a bit stunned."

"Okay," I said, reaching into my pocket and pulling

out my phone. "I'm going to do that now. They need to get here as soon as possible."

I dialed Jake's number and he answered on the third ring. "Charlie."

"I'm at the Maui Diamond. Someone just tried to kill Marion."

"I'll be there in ten minutes. Where are you?"

"Suite 902."

"Is she all right? Do you need an ambulance?"

"No. We're both fine. I think." Marion nodded at me. "Yeah, we're okay. Just... get here quickly, okay?"

"I'll be there as soon as I can."

I hung up the phone and exhaled deeply. Jake was coming. It was all going to be fine.

I sat up, slowly this time, and turned to Marion. "I need you to run me through exactly what happened."

Marion bit her lower lip but nodded. "Yes. Okay. I was here, in the suite, when it happened. I sent Amber out to get us some coffee about twenty minutes ago. She likes a place that's up in Kihei, so it takes her a while. She'll be back soon, I hope. Anyway, I was here by myself. I was just sitting at the kitchen table, answering some e-mails. I've been speaking with... well, I'm afraid I can't tell you just yet. But let's just say I've got some very interesting projects in the pipeline, and I was emailing the director."

Marion shuddered. "Then, there was a noise at the front door. I thought it was Amber. I assumed she'd forgotten her car keys. She'd just left, after all. I didn't think anything of it, and didn't even turn around. But Amber always says hi when she comes in, no matter what.

Always has. And this person didn't. I turned around, and he had a knife. He swiped at me, and I was able to duck out of the way just in time. He grabbed me by the neck. That was when you knocked at the door. I shouted, and he hit me and ran away. By the time I got to the door, you were in the hallway, unconscious. I dragged you inside, then closed and locked the door in case whoever it was came back. I was about to call an ambulance when you woke up."

"So I was only out a couple of minutes?"

Marion nodded. "Yes. It couldn't have been more than that. I'm not strong enough to get you onto the couch, but I didn't want whoever that was coming back. I put the latch across the door, so even if he has a key, he can't get in again. Oh my God. I can't believe it. He came back to kill me. Charlie, you saved my life."

Marion began to pace around the room. Her hands were shaking, and I slowly rose to my feet, trying to blink away the pressure behind my eyes. I looked around the suite. Nothing looked out of place, except for Marion's laptop, which sat on the dining room counter at a slightly unnatural angle, probably knocked a little bit to the side when Marion was trying to evade the attacker.

A tiny smudge of blood was on the edge of the table; that was probably Marion's, but I made a mental note to alert Jake of it nonetheless.

Hopefully hotel security would have footage of the attacker.

Marion was obviously not doing well. Now that the initial adrenaline of the attack had worn off, and what had just happened had sunk in, she appeared to be panicking slightly. Her eyes kept darting toward the door, and she was trembling more than she had been a minute ago.

"Don't touch anything," I told her. "Listen, he wasn't in the bedroom, was he?"

Marion shook her head. "No."

"Come with me. We're going to get you to lie down until Jake gets here, okay? You've had a shock, and you need to relax."

"You shouldn't be taking care of me," Marion protested as I led her toward the enormous French doors that opened to a bedroom the size of my entire apartment. "You were the one who was knocked unconscious."

"I'm fine," I said. And that was mostly true. My head still hurt, but the earth was no longer spinning, and while I could practically feel the bump on the top of my head, as long as I didn't touch it, it didn't hurt too much.

I led Marion to the king-sized bed, and she lay down on top of the covers. I went to the cupboard, grabbed a blanket, and put it over her. I thought I remembered something Zoe said once about keeping people warm after they've had a shock.

Before I had a chance to do anything else, there was a knock at the door. Instantly, my blood ran cold, but a moment later Jake's voice came through.

"Charlie? Marion? It's Jake. I'm here."

I rushed over and opened the door for Jake, who

looked at me with concern in his eyes. "Are you all right?" His voice was soft, softer than normal.

I nodded. "Yes. I put Marion in bed. She was pacing, shaking, obviously not doing well. I think she's in shock."

"What happened?"

"The short version: someone broke in here and tried to kill her. I showed up, and obviously scared him off. He hit me over the head as he left. Marion brought me in here and locked the door behind us. Her assistant should be back soon."

"Amber?"

"Right. Sorry. I forgot, you're also on this case. You know who Amber is."

Jake looked like he was going to say something, even going so far as to open his mouth for a second, then he thought better of it and closed it. Maybe he felt bad for me since I'd been hit over the head. Probably something related to the fact that he was the actual cop on this case investigating, so of course I should have remembered he knew who Amber was.

I was starting to think maybe I had a slight concussion.

"Okay, I need to speak to Marion," Jake said. I led him into the bedroom, where Marion was looking up at the ceiling. Even though she wore barely any makeup this morning, there was still an elegance about her that made her seem not real somehow.

She reached out a hand to Jake when he approached the bed, and he took it. "Thank you so much for coming." Marion sat up in the bed. "It was horrible. Truly horrible. The man attacked me, here in my suite. I thought I was going to die. And then poor Charlie was hit over the head."

"I need you to tell me exactly what happened, as well as you can remember it," Jake said. "It's important."

"Of course. Whatever I can do to help." Marion leaned back against the pillows and began recounting the story, the same one she had told me only a few minutes earlier. I listened in again, in case there were any new pertinent details she could add, but nothing.

"Did the man say anything?" Jake asked when she had finished, and I mentally face-palmed for not having thought of asking that myself.

"Not a word. He let out a little bit of a gasp when he heard Charlie at the door, but that's all. I'm afraid I wouldn't be able to identify him by his voice."

"Did you see what color his eyes were? How tall he was? Anything else about him, physically?"

Marion inhaled sharply as she closed her eyes, lost in the memory of being attacked. "His eyes were the color of a roasted espresso bean, but without the warm expectation of comfort one normally associates with the sight."

I looked over at Jake and raised my eyebrows. Marion was obviously trying to be poetic. I would have just said his eyes were brown.

"He was tall, but not intimidatingly so. Perhaps Charlie has a better idea as to his height. I thought he might have been an inch or two taller than me."

Marion was about five foot ten, which would have

put the man around six feet tall. I nodded. "Yeah, I'd agree with that. He wasn't built thickly, either. I didn't get the best look, since he hit me so quickly, but I got the impression that he was of medium build, maybe even skinny."

"Yes," Marion said, nodding. "I agree."

Jake jotted down the information in his notebook. "All right. I'm going to have a small crime scene unit come here to take fingerprints."

"It won't be any use. He was wearing gloves," Marion said.

"He was," I confirmed. That was one of the things I'd noticed before he'd hit me over the head. Plain, black gloves.

"Nonetheless, I want this place looked over completely," Jake said. "A man came in here to try to kill you. If there is any evidence that might lead to his identity being uncovered, I want to find it."

"Yes, yes. You are right, of course," Marion said quickly. "I only ask that you please bring in the most discreet people you have. I really do hate having my personal life plastered all over the papers, and I'd really rather not see the inside of my suite revealed for all to see."

"I'll take extra steps to ensure your privacy," Jake assured her. "No personal phones will be allowed in this suite, among other things."

"Thank you. I really appreciate everything you're doing to help me. I knew someone was trying to kill me, but frankly, there was a part of me that thought maybe they would have given up after they killed Crystal by accident." Marion shuddered. "Evidently, I was wrong."

Suddenly, the sound of someone trying to enter the suite came from the living room. "Stay here. Don't move," Jake said quietly and headed toward the front door. I followed after him, all too aware that he held one hand on his gun as he approached the door.

"Marion?" a familiar voice called out. "I'm afraid you've locked me out."

"It's Amber," I said quietly, hearing the relief in my own voice.

"What part of 'stay here' sounded like 'follow me to the front door' to you?" Jake asked, shaking his head incredulously. He double-checked that it really was Amber, then opened the safety latch at the top of the door and let her in.

"Detective Llewelyn?" Amber asked, her brow furrowing slightly as she entered, carrying a tray with three coffees. "What's going on? Is there news? Have you found the person who killed Crystal?"

"Marion was attacked after you left," Jake said quietly, and Amber's mouth dropped open as she placed the tray of coffee on the coffee table.

"What?"

"A man broke in here. Charlie's arrival scared him off. They're both going to be fine, but they were very lucky."

"Oh my God. I don't believe it."

"Did you see anybody suspicious on your way out of here? Anyone dressed in all black, maybe?"

Amber shook her head. "No. Not that I noticed.

But then, I wouldn't have really noticed anyone. Marion wanted to get her hair done, so I was scrolling through my phone, trying to find the contact information for the woman she likes to use in Maui. I made sure I didn't walk into anyone on my way to the parking lot, but that was it. I wasn't paying attention to anything else other than my phone."

"Where are Marion's bodyguards?" I asked, suddenly remembering they had been around when we met at the coffee shop.

"They have a room a few floors down," Amber explained. "They're on call, but they only come out when Marion wants to leave the room. We always figured she was safe here."

An expression of helplessness passed over her face.

Jake nodded. "All right. I'd like to speak to them, if possible."

"Of course."

"Right now, I want you to go into the bedroom and take care of Marion, please. Don't touch anything out here."

"I can do that. Um, this coffee is for Charlie. Marion asked me to get one, since you were coming today. Sorry, Detective, I didn't know you'd be here."

"Not a problem," Jake replied, and I took the iced latte from Amber with a grateful smile. It was a nice detail, remembering that I'd had an iced coffee the last time we met. But then, I supposed those were the kinds of details you had to remember if you were the personal assistant to one of the most famous people in Hollywood.

"I'm going to go call in the crime scene people, and see hotel security," Jake said.

"I'm coming with you," I chimed in.

"Absolutely not."

"Oh, please. I'm a victim here. That gives me the right to come with you."

"That isn't how this works."

"I will literally cling to your back like the world's most annoying monkey so you have no choice to take me with you."

"You do realize that's a crime, right?"

"Sure, but if you actually arrested me for it, you'd have to explain to the whole courtroom that you're charging me with assaulting a police officer for basically demanding a piggyback ride. Then who do you think will look silly?"

Jake pressed his palms into his eyes for a moment. "I can't believe you sometimes. Okay, fine. You win. You can come with me to talk to security, but under no circumstances are you to say anything. I'm doing *all* the talking. I know that's probably going to be hard for you."

"Wow, rude much?"

Jake shot me a look. "Do you want me to rescind this offer?"

"No, no. Fine. I won't say anything. I promise."

Jake nodded, and I scurried after him into the hallway.

Chapter 17

"I really need to get myself one of those," I said, motioning with my head to Jake's badge. After flashing it to the woman working at the front counter, we were quickly escorted to the head of security's office. We were currently walking down one of the hallways, with the receptionist about three feet in front of us. I had a feeling if I'd gone down there by myself the conversation would have been a lot more difficult.

"Again, highly illegal."

"Were you just born without a sense of humor, or do they take it away from you when you become a cop?" I asked.

"Gee, I don't know. Why don't you ask your new boyfriend?"

"Oh, is *that* what this is about? You saw the photo of Rowan kissing me on the beach, and now you're jealous, even though there's nothing going on between us?"

"Why would you possibly think that's what's going on here, and not that I'm a detective doing a job and I don't need an untrained civilian behind me?"

"Because you never cared about that before."

"This is not what that's about. I don't care that you're in a relationship with Rowan."

"For what it's worth, I'm not."

Jake turned and raised an eyebrow in my direction. "I saw the picture. It certainly looks like the two of you are in a relationship."

"Well, pictures don't tell the whole story, especially not in gossip magazines. I'm not dating Rowan, not that it's any of your business. I was making Natalie jealous, because she knocked me over while we were doing stand-up paddleboard yoga."

This time, a smile flittered on Jake's lips. "Really?"

"If you must know, yes. Now, get it together. You and me, we're not a couple. If you want to date me, then ask me out for real. If you don't, then that's fine. But either way, you don't get to be short with me just because I'm with someone else when there's nothing going on between us."

"For the record, I was not being short with you because of that. I'm being short with you because someone almost killed you this morning and you don't seem to be doing anything about it."

"What do you want me to do? Hide in the corner? Lie down on the bed like Marion, trembling, and waiting for the killer to come back? This is what I'm doing about it: I'm coming with you to speak to security and find out who it was. Besides, the attacker didn't want me dead. They just didn't want me coming after them."

"You could have still easily been killed," Jake said. "And you're right, you are doing something. I'm sorry."

I raised an eyebrow. "Is that a real apology from Jake Llewelyn?"

"Oh, can it," he said, but the corner of his mouth curled up into a smile as the receptionist stopped in front of a large, wooden door. On it, stenciled in fancy gold letters, was the word "Security," with "Authorized access only" underneath it.

The receptionist pulled out a key card and pressed it against the reader next to the door. The machine beeped and a small green light flashed, and the receptionist opened the door, motioning for us to enter.

"Jesse, I'd like you to meet two detectives from the Maui Police. There's been an incident with Marion Hennessey."

Jesse stepped forward. He was about five foot ten, with a body composition that could best be described as a snowman. Seriously, his head was bald and his face was perfectly round, as was his body, and even his legs were at the very least vaguely oval-shaped. His cheeks were ruddy, and his blue eyes intelligent and bright. He walked over briskly and shook hands first with Jake and then with me.

"It's nice to meet you. You say there's been an incident with Marion Hennessey?"

"I'm Jake Llewelyn, and this is Charlotte Gibson," Jake said, introducing us. "We'd like to speak to you about events that took place this morning."

"Of course. But I haven't been alerted of anything out of the ordinary with Ms. Hennessey's suite. Also, sorry to ask, but could I please see some identification? You have to understand, with guests of Ms. Hennessey's status, security is a top priority."

Jake pulled out his badge and showed it to Jesse, who looked at it then nodded. "All right. What is this about? I haven't been informed of any problems pertaining to the security of Ms. Hennessey's suite."

"She was attacked in it this morning," Jake explained. "She chose to call me first, as I'm the detective in charge of the investigation into Crystal Harris's death."

Jesse's expression immediately turned grim. "Is she all right?"

"She's fine, luckily. But we're hoping to get video footage of the intruder."

"Follow me." Jesse led us to a private office on the left side of the room, with a multiple-monitor setup along one wall. There were no extra chairs on which to sit, but that was fine. Jesse took a seat at the desk that held the main computer connected to the monitors, and Jake and I stood behind him.

"Unfortunately, we don't have any security cameras on the ninth floor. It's to ensure the privacy of our guests who stay here. The ninth-floor penthouses are where all of the rich and famous stay, and they sometimes get up to some things they'd rather not have on video."

"In this case, it would be significantly more useful to us if we did have security footage," Jake pointed out.

"I realize that. And believe me, as head of security, I'd much rather we have security cameras up there. But the guests don't want them, and I'm not the one paying the bills." Jesse shrugged. "Unfortunately, we're limited to the public areas of the resort. And even then, there's no guarantee. The ninth floor has a private entrance. Did the intruder have a key to access the suite?"

"Yes," Jake said. "Is there a log of the keys that are assigned to each suite?"

"Sure is," Jesse said, leaning over with a grunt, and tapped away at the keyboard for a minute. "It looks like there are two keys assigned to Ms. Hennessey's room."

I frowned. "Well, that's one for Marion, and one for Amber. We know she had one since she used it to try and get back into the suite when she came back with coffee, but Marion had put the safety latch on so she couldn't get in. So where did the attacker get one?"

"Which employees would have access to a key that could open that door?" Jake immediately asked.

"I'll get you a list. I'm sure it wasn't any of them, but you're welcome to speak with them. There's the housekeeping staff, of course. Then security. I have one on me right now. And the managers. That's about it. But I'm telling you, no one here did this. Not a chance."

"I'll grab that list of names off you all the same," Jake said. I could tell he didn't take Jesse's word for it whatsoever.

"What about the restaurant or bar staff?" I asked. "Is there any reason any of them would have a copy of a key that could open any door in this place?"

"No, no way," Jesse replied immediately. "Even the managers. They only have keys that allow them access to the restaurant side of the building. There's no reason for them to be able to enter rooms."

"Can we see your lobby footage from the time of the attack?" Jake asked.

"Sure."

Jesse lined up a few angles, and we spent a little while watching the video, but nothing stood out at me.

"I only saw him for a split second," I said apologetically to Jake when we were finished. "I didn't get a good look. I'm not sure I'd recognize him if he was standing here in front of me. Sorry."

Jake nodded. "Totally understandable. I hoped we might get lucky. Any chance I can get this footage on a memory card to show Marion?"

Jesse nodded. "Of course. Whatever I can do to help."

"Who would know about the private entrance?" I asked. "The one to the ninth floor."

"Well, anyone who's stayed there before," Jesse said. "Most of the staff. And anyone who's been told about it. It's not exactly the nuclear codes."

I frowned. That wasn't going to help us narrow it down at all.

Jesse got the footage for Jake, the two exchanged contact information, and Jake and I left the office a moment later.

"I thought you promised you weren't going to say anything," Jake said, raising an eyebrow in my direction as we walked back toward reception.

"They were good questions, though, so you can't be mad," I replied smugly.

"Is that so?"

"That's exactly so. But it sounds like we flunked out with security."

"I hate to admit it, but you're right. It would have been so easy if there had been cameras on the ninth floor, or in the private entrance."

"I wonder what's happened in the past that celebrities don't want getting out," I said.

"My bet, after working a hotel in Waikiki to make rent when I was in college: it's hookers. Definitely hookers."

I blew a raspberry. "Boring."

"And what exactly would you like to see celebrities doing with these hotel rooms?"

"I dunno. Something exciting, something actually worth writing about. Setting things on fire. Committing crimes with a raccoon sidekick. Summoning pirate ghosts from another world in the middle of the night during the full moon."

"There are no racoons in Hawaii."

"I like how *that's* the part you felt the need to point out was unrealistic. Hookers are boring. Everyone knows people pay for sex."

"Yes, but most people don't want it getting out in the papers."

"That's true. Have they considered *not* hiring hookers, if they're rich and famous and their reputation hinges on the entire world not finding out about it?"

"I'm not sure you're in a place to be questioning other people's life decisions," Jake pointed out.

"Now, that's a low blow. What happened this morning isn't my fault."

"No, that's true. But still, you're the only person I know who finds herself in these kinds of situations time and time again."

"That's because I'm basically Batman, only better looking."

Jake snorted. "I'm going to chalk that one up to the hit to your head this morning."

"Okay. Mean comments about me not being Batman aside, what do you think about this? The intruder knew the routine. He knew that Amber was in there with Marion, and waited for her to leave before he struck. At least, I think we should assume that's the case."

"I agree. It would be too much of a coincidence that he just happened to enter just a couple of minutes after Marion's assistant left. Whoever did this wasn't an idiot and knew at least some of Marion's schedule." Then Jake asked pointedly, "What do you think about Amber?"

"You're thinking because it all happened after she left?" I asked, and Jake nodded. I bit my lip as I considered my reply. "The only motive we've found for Amber is her hidden Instagram account."

"Really?"

I grinned. "Oh, I forgot, you're not as good at this as I am."

Jake scowled, but I continued. "We found a secret

Instagram account Amber is keeping. Basically, she just rants about Marion and how she's actually demanding and mean. But to be honest, I don't think it's murder-worthy. It's just somebody complaining into the void about her boss. The account has no followers, and doesn't follow anyone back. It's also set to private."

"Then how did you get access?"

I wiggled my eyebrows. "A girl's got to be able to have her secrets. Anyway, the important thing is, I don't think Amber has any real motive to do this. Although that said, she does have a key to Marion's suite."

"Yes. That list of employees should be interesting. I tend to agree with you, though. This was someone who knew Marion's schedule. Someone who knew her habits, who was close to her. This doesn't read to me as some random crazy who works for the hotel."

"Someone like an ex-husband?" I asked.

"Maybe. Have you spoken to Jamieson yet?"

I shook my head. "No. In fact, that was one of the reasons I was here this morning. Marion is going to organize it for me. We can't all just flash a badge and get whatever we want."

"Is that what you think most of my job is?"

"Like, a solid ninety percent of it, yeah," I said playfully.

Jake laughed. "Maybe not *quite* that much. Anyway, I spoke to Bill yesterday. Nothing he said has me ruling him out as a suspect yet."

"What did he tell you?"

"Do you think if you just ask me for confidential

police information a hundred times over, I'll just give up and tell you?"

"Honestly? That's the strategy I'm with right now."

"I can tell you right now it's not going to work. A guy has to have his secrets, after all."

"We'll have to see about that."

"I was in the Navy. I've literally been trained to withstand torture by captors."

"Yeah, well, the Navy never prepared you for Charlie Gibson, did it?" I asked, shooting him a wink.

Jake laughed. "You've got that right."

"So, what did Bill Jamieson tell you?"

"The answer is still no."

Chapter 18

We reached Marion's suite then. The door was open, and a few members of a crime scene unit were inside, scouring the place for any physical evidence that might have been missed. I didn't get my hopes up. One man was getting the blood from the kitchen counter.

"She's in the bedroom," one of the investigators said to Jake, who thanked him.

When we entered, Marion was still on the bed. She held the cup of coffee in both hands, while Amber was on the phone.

"Yes. Noon our time will work just fine. Thank you."

Amber hung up the phone and looked at us. "Do you know who did it?"

"Not yet," Jake replied. "We have footage from the lobby. Charlie was unable to identify anybody, but Marion, we'd like you to have a look as well."

"Anything I can do," Marion said, her voice barely more than a whisper.

Jake turned to Amber. "Do you have an iPad here by any chance?"

"Sure. Let me grab it."

She returned a moment later, and Jake connected an adapter he had in his pocket to the iPad, allowing him to load up the files from the thumb drive that Jesse had given him.

Jake handed the iPad to Marion, who put down her coffee to watch the video. Amber stepped out of the bedroom into the main living room, and I followed after her.

"I know about your private Instagram account," I said quietly, so no one else could hear. Amber paused, pressing her lips together and closing her eyes.

"You can't tell Marion."

"Don't worry, I won't."

"I just needed somewhere to vent, okay? Like, the reality is, she's a good boss. I do like my job. It's just that sometimes, she's a lot. She's a celebrity, and she lets it get to her head. Sometimes she takes it out on me, and I vent on my secret account. How did you find it, anyway? It's supposed to be private. It has zero followers."

"Always assume that nothing on the internet is private."

"Yeah. I guess so. Look, I'm going to delete it. Today. Please just don't tell her about it."

"I don't intend to. But you have to know how it looks, given this investigation."

Amber inhaled sharply. "Do you really think I'd kill her because she called me a bitch? Before this job, I worked retail. Do you know how much worse that was? I had a customer follow me into the parking lot and threaten me because I told her we didn't have the specific American Girl doll she wanted in stock. So yeah, I'm not going to kill Marion over anything she did. But I might just rant about it on my private account. I don't even use her name."

Amber's hands fidgeted as her eyes darted around. She was obviously terrified of being outed here.

"It's okay," I said. "I believe you."

Amber breathed a sigh of relief. "Thank you. You have no idea how terrified I've been that someone would find the account. I wanted to tell the police and you all about it, but then I thought it would make me look guilty, so I decided to keep it to myself and hope it would never be uncovered. I didn't know what to do."

"Yeah. I mean, it doesn't cast you in a great light, all things considered, but I believe you that it was just you letting off steam. I've worked crappy jobs before. I know what it's like."

"And this one honestly isn't the worst I've ever had. When I worked at Walmart, I ran a meme page for employees to share their worst horror stories."

"Oh, yikes. That had to be bad."

"You have no idea how many people poop in the aisles."

I scrunched up my face. "I don't want to know."

"It's a lot," Amber whispered with a nervous giggle. "Anyway, I want to find the person who did this as much as you do. I mean it. Marion is good to me, overall. Besides, I'd rather be yelled at in Hawaii than doing literally anything in Los Angeles. I don't want to lose this job, and if she dies, well, that's it."

"Okay. I need to get in touch with her ex-husband. That's one of the things I came here to speak with her about."

"Bill? Why do you have to talk to him? He's not even on the island."

"He is, though. He was at the restaurant the night Crystal was killed."

Amber's eyes widened. "Oh, geez."

"Yeah."

"You think he might have done this?"

"What do you think?"

"No question. Bill has a temper. I've seen him yell at Marion multiple times. The two are really bad for one another. Their relationship is super toxic. If you asked me who I thought was most likely to kill Marion, I'd have said him, but I didn't know he was even on the island. What is he doing here?"

"I'm hoping to find out when I speak to him."

"Yeah, of course." Amber pulled out her phone and tapped away at it for a moment. "Here's his number."

She handed it to me, and I recorded the number off the screen into my own phone. "Thanks."

"You'll just get his assistant. He refuses to take any calls from Marion or from me directly, and patches us through to Anna every time. She hates him, though. Tell her you're trying to put Bill in jail, and she'll organize a meeting for you quick as a flash."

I chuckled. "Good to know."

"I wish I'd seen someone on the way out, you know," Amber said with a sigh. "I keep running over everything in my head. If someone attacked Marion… do you think I'm in danger?"

I pursed my lips. "I'd be lying if I said no. I was hoping whoever was trying to kill Marion had given up after failing the first time, but that's obviously not the case. I think anyone who's near her for long periods of time is at risk."

Amber sighed. "Damn. I get paid well, but not well enough to be killed. At least he didn't have a gun."

"Yeah, I'm pretty happy about that too."

Jake emerged from the bedroom and headed toward us. "Anything?" I asked.

Jake shook his head. "No. I think we've hit a dead end. I've spoken to Marion about making sure she has extra security around her at all times these days."

"Okay. I'm going to head off. I have some more stuff to do today for another case, and I need to speak with Bill."

"Are you sure you don't need to get checked out?" Jake asked.

"I'm fine. It was a little hit over the head, that's all. It's not like he shot me. But thanks. When Zoe comes home, I'll have her give me a once-over, just in case."

"Good. Take care of yourself. It's okay to rest."

"Not while there's a murderer out there."

I said goodbye to Jake and Amber and headed back

down to the lot where I'd left Queenie. I sat in the driver's seat for a minute, inhaling the warm, fresh air of the day and letting the sun's rays beat down on me. There was barely a cloud in the sky today, and a mynah bird nearby chirped a happy song.

I'd been attacked. It hadn't really sunk in just yet, not fully. That man had come out of Marion's apartment and knocked me unconscious. He could have killed me so easily. I had to find who it was, and fast.

I put the key in the ignition and began the slow meander back to South Kihei Drive as I headed to Dot's apartment. The more I thought about it, the more convinced I was that it had to be someone at that table, or Bill. It wouldn't have been one of the kitchen staff. The person who did this knew Marion. They knew her habits. They knew how to get to the ninth-floor apartment.

There were a few key questions I didn't have answers to. For one, where did they get a key to enter? The only two people who had keys were Marion and Amber. Obviously, it wasn't Marion's key which was used. That left Amber, and I was pretty sure she was innocent. I just didn't have a motive for her, beyond hating her boss, but lots of people hated their bosses without murdering them. And she was right, this job was, all things considered, better than cleaning up poop in the aisles of big box stores. But if I found a motive, she definitely had the means and opportunity. She could have very easily left the apartment, slipped her key to the attacker, and either hung around for him to bring it back to her, or just had him drop it off somewhere and grabbed it on her way back from getting the coffee. Plus, she would have been able to tell him exactly where the private entrance was, where he wouldn't have been seen.

The second question, which I hadn't asked anyone else yet, was why bring a knife? A gun would have been much more useful. A knife involved having to get close to the person being attacked. It carried more risk, as was proven by the attacker running off when I knocked at the door. Could it be as simple as the killer didn't have access to a gun? I mean, come on, as much as some tourists didn't realize it, Hawaii was still part of the United States. It really wasn't that hard to get a gun here.

A knife was a much more personal way to kill someone. You had to get close to them. You had to basically look them in the eye. It was the sort of thing an ex-husband would use to kill someone he really, truly hated.

When I pulled into Dorothy's building's parking lot and slid into one of the visitor spots, I pulled out my phone and dialed the number Amber had given me for Bill Jamieson.

"Good morning, Anna speaking," a voice on the other end of the line said. She couldn't have possibly sounded more bored.

"Hi, Anna. This is Charlie Gibson. I got your number from Amber, Marion's assistant."

"Oh, hello. You're that investigator trying to find out who killed Crystal, aren't you? I saw your picture on TMZ."

"That's me."

"Well, what can I do for you?"

"I need to speak to Bill about what happened that night. Can you set up a meeting with him for me?"

"Absolutely, especially if you're trying to throw his ass in jail," Anna purred in reply, and it was all I could do not to laugh. Amber was right. Anna really was not shy about how much she didn't like her boss.

"If he's the killer, then yeah, that's the goal."

"Does this afternoon work for you? I can slot you in at four."

"Sure, that's great."

"Perfect. Let me give you the address."

I jotted down the information, then thought I'd see what kind of information I could get from Anna. "Hey, can I ask you something?"

"Shoot."

"Where was Bill this morning?"

"Sorry, wouldn't have a clue."

"He didn't have any meetings or anything?"

"Nope. His whole schedule was clear. But then, he's on vacation. That's the whole point of those things, is taking time off. Not that *I* get to have any time off. Apparently, I'm too important. He can't possibly call his dermatologist to make his monthly appointment himself even once. Or figure out how his Uber Eats app works. Sometimes, I swear, it's like working for a freaking monkey. No, that's an insult to monkeys. I'm sure some scientist somewhere has given one an iPhone, and it can figure out how to order Shake Shack on its own."

I snorted. I immediately liked Anna. "So, how easy would it be for Bill to get access to Botox? Like, theoretically."

"Honey, you've obviously never been to LA. They give that shit away as samples at Costco over there."

"I know you're exaggerating for effect, but you have no idea how desperately I want that story to be true. It's everything I ever expected Los Angeles to be. So, you're saying Bill could easily access Botox."

"Oh, no question. He gets injections regularly when we're back home, as much as he denies it. I'm sure he could find some on Maui if he wanted to." Anna's voice turned into the hushed whisper of a woman looking for gossip. "Why? Do you think he used Botox to kill that yoga instructor?"

"I'm afraid I can't say right now. I'm looking at him, though. He was at the restaurant that night."

"Yes. I'm the one who made the reservation for him. He wanted to sit at the bar."

"A reservation? How early did you make it?"

Anna hummed for a moment on the other end of the line, thinking back. "It was that morning, maybe? I told him not to worry about it, that he was Bill Jamieson, and that he never seemed to have any trouble dropping his own name when it suited him, but he insisted."

"Did he say why?"

A cold laugh came from the other end of the line. "Bill? Not a chance. I'm not important enough to be told why he does anything."

"But he definitely wanted a table at the bar that day, for four o'clock."

"No question. He asked for it himself, and I booked it personally."

"Cool, thanks. Good to know." I jotted down the information. I didn't know what it meant just yet, but it might be important.

"Yeah. Honestly, if you throw the guy in jail, you'll be doing me a favor."

"Look, I have to ask. If you hate him so much, why do you keep this job?"

Anna laughed on the other end of the line. "You know, people rarely ask me that to my face. Truth is, as bad as Bill is, I've actually had worse jobs. Here, I usually just pick up the phone, make appointments, deal with the entitled Hollywood elite who believe they're owed a piece of Bill's time. But the thing is, I hate all of them. I hate Bill, but the rest of them are exactly the same, with a few exceptions. Never meet celebrities. As much as they claim it doesn't, they *totally* let the fame go to their heads. So, I don't let them through unless Bill wants them to. And he appreciates that I'm able to tell them exactly where they can shove their Emmys and Oscars, so he pays me well. If one day I lose this job, well, so be it. But for now, it's where I am, and I do it well, so Bill puts up with the quirkier aspects of my personality."

I laughed, shaking my head. "I'm impressed."

"Yeah, I'm pretty great."

"Okay, thanks for the help. You've got my number. If you think of anything else that might help me prove

Bill killed that lady—or if he didn't—can you let me know?"

"Sure. Will do. Have a good one, Charlie."

"You too."

I hung up the phone and stared at the black screen for a little bit, trying to make sense of the assistant I'd just met. Anna was certainly something, and I'd made a note of what she had to say, but I wasn't sure it was going to make a difference either way.

At least this afternoon I was meeting Bill Jamieson. Hopefully I would have a better idea as to whether or not he was a killer.

But for now, this case had to go on the back burner. There was nothing I could do anymore, and I wanted to see what Dot had found out about John Waters, the boring lawyer who was too much of a coward to admit to his wife he'd lost his job six months ago.

Chapter 19

"How's the newfound celebrity going?" Rosie asked with a warm smile as I walked through the door.

"Please don't tell me there are any new photos of me on the internet," I replied. "It's been an interesting morning. Someone attacked Marion. I interrupted them, and he hit me over the head on his way out."

Rosie's mouth dropped open. "Oh, no. I'm glad you're all right."

"Yeah, I'm fine. Just got a bit of a goose egg on the top of my head."

"Let's get some ice on that," Rosie said, heading to the kitchen. "Dot might keep her fridge stocked as badly as a frat house freshman, but it means there's always ice in here."

"I add it to my wine," Dot said with a grin from her spot at the computer.

Rosie rummaged through the kitchen until she

finally emerged with a thin reusable grocery bag—plastic bags were banned on Maui—and dumped a bunch of ice into it. She handed it to me, and I winced as I pressed it against the bump on my head.

Within a few seconds, though, as the cold penetrated my skull, the pain began to ebb, though I wasn't sure if it was because of the ice's healing powers or because the cold was numbing the nerve endings in my head.

Either one was fine with me.

"Did the police catch the person who attacked you?" Rosie asked.

I shook my head. "No. I was knocked unconscious. Marion dragged me into her suite and locked the door behind us, then when I woke up, I called Jake. We looked into it, but so far, it's not looking promising."

"It's interesting, isn't it?" Rosie mused. "What stands out to you about the attack?"

"Well for one thing, whoever wants Marion dead is getting a bit more brazen about it. And he obviously hasn't been put off by the police investigation. It's one thing to try to poison a woman at a bar; it's entirely another to break into her suite and try to stab her to death after her assistant has been sent out for coffee."

"That's Amber, the woman who ran the Instagram account complaining about Marion, right?" Dot asked.

"Yup. I spoke to her about the account. I know she could just be a great actress, but I really believe her when she says she had nothing to do with this. She admitted everything about the Instagram account. It was her, she just wanted to do it to blow off steam and never thought anyone would see the private account, let alone link it to her. After she found out someone was trying to kill Marion she began to worry that if she admitted to running the account she would become a suspect. I do believe her, but I won't erase her off the suspect list completely. I have a meeting with Bill Jamieson this afternoon, which I'm looking forward to. I'd like to know where he was this morning. Anyway, have you found anything else about John Waters?"

"A few things that have potential," Dot said. "Rosie's been listening to the police scanners all morning. The rangers reported him as having not returned to his car, so now the cops have a BOLO out on him. Not that I expect that'll add up to much. What I did find, however, was this."

I leaned forward to get a good look at the screen. It looked like Dot just had a maps app open, with a red dot somewhere just off Lahaina.

"What's that?"

"The last known location of a boat belonging to John Waters's seemingly only friend, another lawyer who worked at his firm."

"How did you find that out?"

"Rosie made some phone calls."

"I'm very good at getting information from people," Rosie said with a smile as she got herself a drink of water from the fridge. "Initially, I just wanted to know who John might have been close to, because I wanted to know about his hiking habits. But one person stood out to me. Nathan Sullivan. He sounded too nervous when I was simply asking him if John liked to hike. So we looked into him as well."

"Nathan Sullivan, partner at the law firm where Waters worked. Didn't burn out like his buddy, but by all accounts, the two of them were good friends, and played a weekly game of squash together. When I looked into his finances, I found a boat. Rosie has a theory about it."

Dot turned to Rosie, who nodded. "Now, what do we know about John Waters? First of all, the man is a coward. He couldn't even tell his wife he lost his job. He's not the sort of man who would have the mental fortitude to commit suicide, even by exposure. Now, he could have gone up to the crater to actually hike, but nobody that I spoke to considered John an outdoor enthusiast. So, why did he suddenly decide to go on a strenuous overnight hike, in late winter, when it's not something he's used to? It's not even a hike that's considered to have a traditionally nice view, like some of the others on the island. So why was he there? I asked Dot for details on the family's finances."

"She knows what she's doing, this one. I looked into it. John's been doing a lot of work moving money between accounts, refinancing his house, that sort of thing, but he was running out of cash, and fast. If I had to guess, he'll make it through to the end of this month, and *maybe* the next before the banks start coming after him. And then the jig's up. He'll have to tell his wife."

"Let me guess," I said, snapping my fingers. "There's a life insurance policy at play here."

"Bingo," Dot said with a grin. "It took me a bit to

find it, since it wasn't registered with his regular banks, but it's there. Ten million dollars, going to his wife if he's dead. But there's a catch: he kills himself, no money."

"But if he dies on the crater because he went hiking without equipment, that's fair game," I said. "But Rosie doesn't think he did that."

"No, I don't. But what's better than actually dying?"

"Faking your own death and then taking your friend's boat to South America, where you can start a new life without anyone being the wiser, and your wife and daughter live the rest of their lives in comfort, crying into their pile of ten million dollars over your death?"

"Great minds think alike," Rosie said with a wink. "It didn't take us long to find Nathan Sullivan's boat, and we suspect that's where John is currently hiding out."

"There's a storm passing through the Pacific right now, right where he'd be traveling, so he's going to have to wait a day or two before he can leave the island safely. As Rosie says, I get the impression John isn't much of an adventurous guy, so he's not going to risk traveling through that."

"What kind of boating experience does he have? Is he even going to make it to South America?"

"Well, he should make it to Mexico," Dot said with a shrug. "Hurricane season won't have started yet, and it's a pretty easy cruise this time of year. As much as traveling thousands of miles by boat in open water can be, anyway. Nathan Sullivan's boat is big, top-of-the-line, and has enough equipment that he should get there no problem as long as he doesn't do anything super dumb. But we're not going to let him get to that point."

"Right. Okay, we have to go talk to him."

"I was hoping you'd say that," Dot said, grinning.

"HOW DO YOU KNOW SO MUCH ABOUT SAILING, anyway?" I called out to Dot in the back seat as I drove Queenie up toward Lahaina.

"Google," she replied. "Plus, you pick it up a bit, just living on Maui for this long. When I dated that guy in Alaska when I was twenty-two, he owned a boat. But the relationship didn't last the winter, and I wasn't about to go out in the ocean there in January."

"No, I don't blame you," I said with a chuckle.

"You'd think it was an entirely different ocean, looking at it. The Pacific in Alaska is *angry*. It really has no spirit of aloha."

"Would you sail to Mexico or California or somewhere if given the opportunity?" I asked.

"Of course I would. Especially if it was after faking my own death. I'd have a few months' worth of alcohol on board, and just let her fly."

Rosie snorted.

"Oh, and I bet you've gone on sailing trips before."

"You forget where I grew up. Your angry Pacific Ocean is where we learned to be in the water. I knew how to pilot a submarine in the Arctic Ocean while you were learning basic calculus."

"I know that's supposed to be a humblebrag, but I feel like neither one of those two examples are things that actually come up in daily use, unless you're James Bond or a math professor."

Before Rosie had a chance to reply, I turned off the highway and began driving down toward the wharf.

"The boat is moored a little ways off land," Dot said.

"Great. That's just what I wanted, more time on the water. Here I was just hoping we'd be able to hop onto the boat directly from the dock."

"Sorry, no such luck. But I have a friend in the area who's going to lend us a dinghy to take out. The mooring isn't far."

"That sounds more stable than a stand-up paddle-board, at least."

"Besides, we're doing a good thing. We're going to make sure John Waters is still alive."

"You're right," I said, miraculously finding a spot in the free parking lot as someone else pulled out. The three of us hopped out of the Jeep and headed to the wharf, where a man who looked like a very out-of-place Santa Claus waved to us from an inflatable dinghy designed to look like a giant floating banana.

"I guess it was too much to ask for you to know anybody normal," I muttered to Dot as I took in the scene. The man at the back of the boat, running the motor, was topless, exposing a hairy chest and badly sunburned shoulders. His head was bare, save for a thick, white beard that reached at least six inches past his chin, and he wore an oversized pair of red Hawaiian-print board shorts.

The boat looked like he'd designed and painted it himself, and there was no way any authority would have actually deemed this craft to be water safe. In fact, I had a sneaking suspicion the duct tape around the front end of the banana boat was the only thing stopping the whole thing from sinking.

Hey, at least it was shaped like a banana which had been split open, and we weren't all going to have to straddle it to try to get to Nathan Sullivan's boat.

"Dottie," Sunburned Santa said, steering the boat up close to the dock. He had a thick Irish accent, and his face broke into a broad smile. "How's me favorite lassie in all the land doing today? Out there breaking legs and hearts?"

"Always," Dot replied with a smile. "Thanks for giving us a hand here today, Liam."

"Of course. I was going out on the water anyway. It's a beautiful day for a sail. Hop on in."

For a split second, I wondered if Dot was going to need a hand getting onto the boat, but of course, that was ridiculous. She deftly dropped into the inflatable banana like it was nothing, followed closely by Rosie. That left me, the youngest of the bunch, carefully sitting on the edge of the dock and dropping in last, looking far less elegant than my two friends.

I sat down on the floor of the boat, since it didn't really have any seats, and settled in for a comfortable ride before we reached Nathan Sullivan's boat.

"All right, here we go," Liam announced, and the motor sprang to life. I yelped and grabbed the side of the inflatable as we did a sharp one-eighty and zoomed out of the harbor. I didn't know what kind of motor Liam had attached to this boat, but it was *powerful.*

Ocean water sprayed up the side from the sheer force of the boat's hull cutting through the waves, and the wind whipped my hair into a frenzy. I grabbed a rope on the edge of the boat and hung on for dear life as Liam cackled with laughter, obviously enjoying the ride.

Rosie sat at the bow, her phone in one hand, occasionally glancing down at it, while Dot was at the stern, talking to Liam. The sound of the motor and the waves quickly drowned out the sound of their conversation, and I found myself looking out at the blue expanse of ocean, trying to spot Nathan's boat. Were we right? Was this where John Waters was hiding? We were about to find out.

Chapter 20

Dot had been right; the mooring point for Nathan's boat wasn't far offshore at all, and it only took about five minutes of cruising in the banana dinghy before we reached it. Cursive lettering on the side of the hull told me the boat was named *The Codfather.* Cute.

About forty, maybe fifty feet long, the catamaran was large, and certainly looked like it could make the voyage from here to Mexico. My eyes scanned the deck, but there was no sign of life. Of course, that didn't necessarily mean John Waters wasn't on this boat; he could have simply been in the cabin.

Liam cut the motor and let the boat glide toward the catamaran. At the back, a ladder was down, leading to the water, and we approached it. I was closest, so I grabbed the ladder, and Rosie grabbed a rope and climbed the ladder before attaching the dinghy to the large catamaran. With the two boats safely anchored to one another, I climbed the ladder next, hoisting myself over the rail and dropping onto the wooden deck.

Dot followed after me a moment later, and I looked down to see if Liam was going to join us, but no. He had already pulled out a fishing rod and was apparently happy to wait until we were finished to give us a ride back to land.

Dot and I moved along the port side of the deck, while Rosie immediately went starboard. We reached the cabin at the same time, where sure enough, John was lying on an upholstered bench, snoring away, a couple of empty beer cans at his side.

"John," Rosie said loudly, and he snorted awake, immediately sitting up as soon as he spotted us.

"Who the hell are you?" he snapped, looking around as if trying to find a weapon. "This boat is private property."

"Relax, we're not here to hurt you, John," Rosie said soothingly.

"How do you know my name? What are you doing here?"

"Your wife hired me to find you," I said quietly. "She's very worried about you. She loves you, John. She loves you very much."

"How did you find me?"

"It's a long story. But listen, we know everything. We know you were laid off, and you couldn't find another job. We know you've been hiding it from your wife, and that you're almost out of money. We know you have that life insurance policy worth ten million, and that your plan was to fake your own death so she could collect the money."

John gaped at me. He didn't look a thing like the professional, put-together lawyer whose pictures I'd seen online anymore. His gray hair was unkempt, like he hadn't brushed it in a couple of days, and a thin layer of stubble grew on his face. He wore a plain gray T-shirt with a frayed collar, and shorts.

"How do you know all this?"

"Again, I'm an investigator, hired by your wife to find you."

"Please," John begged suddenly. "Don't tell her. Don't tell her I'm here. Can you... can you just leave? Get back on your boat, and pretend you were never here. Vanessa needs the money. She's going to need it, more than she's going to need me."

"You don't know that's true. She loves you, John," I said.

"No. No, she might love me, but it's because she doesn't know the truth." Suddenly, tears began flowing from John's eyes. "I was a coward. I didn't dare tell her when I was laid off. Vanessa was so proud of me. I was a lawyer at one of the most prestigious firms on the island. I'd given her a good life, and my daughter too. We were happy, and I lost it all. I couldn't tell her. She wouldn't love me anymore. How could she love someone like me? At first, I figured I'd get another job easily. But it wasn't easy, and the more time passed, the more I lost hope. Eventually, I realized there was no more space for an unemployed lawyer in his fifties, well past his prime. That was it for me. But I didn't have enough of a retirement. I wasn't ready. I wanted to keep Vanessa living the same lifestyle as she was used to, and I couldn't do it anymore. What were my options? I can't do menial work, serving tourists for a low wage. That wouldn't even cover the mortgage payment. Besides, I'm not twenty anymore. I don't *want* to sit behind a cash register all day. I'm a lawyer, for goodness sake. But what do I do when no one will hire me as one? I didn't want to die. Besides, if I committed suicide, Vanessa wouldn't get the money. No, I needed to disappear, but make everyone think I was dead."

"So you finally went to Nathan for help."

"He has this boat. I begged him to let me take it. He wasn't going to, initially. He wanted to lend me enough money to tide me over, but I convinced him it was no use. No law firm on this island was going to hire me. I knew I was a mediocre lawyer. I didn't have the drive to work a hundred hours a week and make partner anywhere. Eventually, Nathan agreed. He gave me the keys to the boat. Said he wouldn't report it stolen for a few months, long enough to get me to Mexico and start a new life. It would never be traced to me."

"That's it then, is it?" Rosie asked. "You give up on life? You give up on ever seeing your family again? You'll never walk your daughter down the aisle. Never hold your grandchildren. Leave your wife to get old alone. She'll die in a hospital bed with no one next to her. You do realize that, don't you?"

John's face fell. "There's no other way. They'll get

over it. I'd rather they think I was dead than know what kind of a man I really am."

"A coward?" Rosie asked.

"Yes," John said quietly. "A coward. That's all I am."

"I've never heard such a load of bull in my life," Rosie said.

John looked up, confused. "What do you mean? It's all true."

"You know what's true? That you're in a bad situation. But you know who goes through tough situations? *Everyone*. Including you. You raised a daughter. You did a good enough job that she's now getting an Ivy League education. You went to law school. You got a good job. You were a practicing lawyer for thirty years. And now you mean to tell me you're going to give it all up because you had a tough year? That's crap, and I won't hear of it."

"No one will hire me," John whined. "I can't do anything if I'm not practicing."

"Name every firm you applied at," Dot ordered. "Go on, we'll wait."

"Well, I spoke to Jenny Lim at her firm, but she wasn't hiring anyone. She did tell me she'd keep me in mind if something came up in the future, but I haven't heard from her since," John said. "That was four months ago. And there was Kekoa, from Kelekolio and Sons. He wasn't looking either."

"And?" Dot asked.

"What do you mean, and?"

"Is that it? Everyone you spoke to?"

John looked down at the ground, obviously embarrassed. "I mean, when they told me no, I figured that was it for me, you know? If they didn't want me, no one else will."

I could practically *feel* Rosie trying to stop herself from rolling her eyes next to me. "So, you asked two people for a job, they said no, and because of that you're giving up, faking your own death, and going to Mexico?"

"Seriously, you're taking this whole midlife crisis thing *way* too far," Dot said, shaking her head.

"This isn't a midlife crisis," John snapped. "It's an *actual* crisis."

"No, it isn't. Get in our boat, come back to shore. Tell your wife what actually happened. She loves you, John. She doesn't love your job. She doesn't love your money. It's obvious that she loves *you*. Just be honest. Then, go out, and ask more than two people for a job. Yeah, it sucks. But guess what, that's life. Sometimes it sucks. You don't get to fake your own death and move to Mexico because you got thrown a little hurdle."

"This is more than just a little hurdle. I'm just not cut out for any of this," John whined.

"Does your daughter really deserve that?" Rosie asked.

"She deserves to believe her father was a good person."

"No, she deserves to have you in her life. Don't you want to be in her life?"

"Of course I do. But I want her to be proud of me."

"Then be someone she can be proud of. Get back out there. Don't run away from your life. Grab it by the horns. There are jobs out there for lawyers. And if not, start your own firm. Come on. You're a middle-aged white man in America, there's nothing you can't do."

This was one hell of a pep talk. Even I was half tempted to go off and start my own law firm. Unfortunately, it didn't have quite the same effect on John.

John moaned. "I can't do it. I just can't."

"You can," Rosie said firmly. "You have no other options here. Do you really think we're going to let you escape to Mexico now? First of all, that would be suborning insurance fraud. And secondly, Charlie was hired by Vanessa. That's where her loyalties lie, not to you. She's going to leave this boat and go tell your wife what's really going on, no matter what you decide. Regardless of what you do, your family will know the truth."

John's face fell. "Don't tell her. Please, don't tell her. I'm begging you. She can't know about this."

"Sorry," Rosie said with a shrug. "Nothing I can do about it."

John's eyes darted around the cabin before landing on me. "You're Charlie, right?"

"That's me. And no, there's nothing you can do to convince me otherwise. I'm going to tell Vanessa what I know, because she's the one who hired me. I suggest you do as Rosie says. She's never steered me wrong before."

"No," John said. "No, I can't."

He jumped up from his seat and ran toward me, a

crazed look in his eyes. I steeled myself, ready to take him on if I needed to, but instead John ran right past me, out onto the boat's deck, where he threw himself over the railing.

The three of us rushed after him, and I sprinted to the edge of the boat, grabbing onto the railing and looking down at the water below.

John was thrashing about in the water, while Liam hooted with glee. "I caught one," he called out to us, managing to wink in our direction. He yanked on his fishing rod, which looked like it was hooked on John's board shorts.

"Reel him in, then, sailor," Dot called out, and Liam did as ordered. I was surprised nothing on the fishing rod snapped as he dragged John toward the boat. When John was close enough for Liam to reach him, the older man dropped the rod on the floor of the boat, reached over, grabbed John by the T-shirt, and dragged him spluttering into the bottom of the boat.

"Now, that wasn't very smart of you, was it, my boy?" Liam asked as John coughed up seawater.

John looked up at us as he finally settled himself down. "Why are you here? Why couldn't you just leave well enough alone? You just had to meddle, didn't you?"

"Yes," I said, heading back to the ladder and climbing into the boat. "Because believe me, I know a thing or two about starting again. It's a lot harder than you think it's going to be. Do you even speak Spanish?"

John looked at me like I was crazy. "No. But it's Mexico. It's fine, people will speak English."

"Sure, at first. And how do you expect to make money?"

"I... don't know," John admitted. "I had five thousand dollars Nathan gave me. That would buy me some time to figure it out."

"Not as long as you think," Rosie said as she dropped effortlessly into the boat herself, followed closely by Dot.

"Picking up your whole life and starting over can be great, but it can also suck. I know. I've done it. And you do not seem to me to be the kind of guy who can fight through the issues you're going to come up against. This is stupid. We're all going to go back to your home, you're going to admit everything to Vanessa, she's going to take you back if you're lucky, and you're going to solve the problems you have now, on this island, instead of escaping to Mexico and creating new problems there. Got it?"

John looked like he wanted to argue, but he was obviously a man who had given up. Maybe hitting him in the face with the reality of starting over completely in a foreign country where he didn't have any sort of safety net—or even his own identity—had finally got him to come to his senses.

"Okay," he muttered. "Fine. You win. But... what am I going to do? How am I going to do this?"

"You're going to tell the truth," Rosie said firmly. "We're going to take you to see Vanessa, and you're going to tell her everything. And she might forgive you. She might not. It might be the end of your marriage. But whatever Vanessa decides to do, you will move on."

"You're gonna be all right no matter what happens, my man," Liam said. "I've been married seven times. So it doesn't work out the first time, it's no big deal."

This didn't look like much of a comfort to John. Dot unhooked the boat from the ladder, and we headed off to shore, John sitting on the floor of the boat with his head between his knees, looking like he was going to puke, and it had nothing to do with seasickness.

Chapter 21

When we reached the shore, the three of us basically frog-marched John back to Queenie.

"We need to get him some nicer clothes," I said as we walked down Front Street and back toward the car. "And possibly a shower. Not that it's going to change the fact that he lied to his wife for almost a year, but it would probably help if she can focus on his words and not that he hasn't showered in three days."

"Good call," Dot said with a nod.

An hour later, thanks to the public showers at one of the nearby beaches, and a quick stop at a couple of menswear stores on Front Street, John looked more or less like a functional human being once again. The three of us drove off in the direction of Kahului, to get to John's house near Kula.

"I just don't know what I'm doing anymore," John said as we drove down the highway. Kula was nearly an hour away. "The last time I had to look for a job, I was just out of law school. Everyone I knew was in the same situation I was, and we were all giving each other a hand, you know? But how do you start again at fifty? Do you know how embarrassing it is, going to your peers, people you've known for twenty-five, thirty years, and telling them you're out of work while they're out making partner? It's humiliating."

"Do you think you're the first person to ever lose their job? Do you think you're the first unemployed person your colleagues have ever met? No, of course not," Dot said to him. "The situation isn't ideal. But you deal with it, and you move on. You don't wallow for six months and then decide the solution is to fake your own death."

"Look, it sounded like a good idea at the time. Still does, frankly. If it weren't for you meddlers, I'd be just about on my way. I was supposed to leave tomorrow."

"This is the closest I've ever come in my life to being part of a real-life *Scooby-Doo* moment," I said with a grin. "I always wanted to be Daphne."

"Oh? Who do you think we are, then?" Dot asked.

"Well, Rosie is obviously Velma."

"No argument there."

"And you're Shaggy through and through. Only hotter."

"I've never smoked weed in my life." Dot glared at me, as if I'd insulted her very being.

"There are no words to describe how little I believe that statement."

"Okay, maybe once or twice," Dot admitted with a cheeky smile.

"Your situation isn't hopeless," Rosie said, interrupting Dot and my *Scooby-Doo* chat. "You have applied for jobs at two firms so far, and I'm going to go out on a limb and say you probably didn't do it well. I have a friend who works in recruitment on this island. I'll put you in touch with him. He'll find you a position that's suitable for you, I'm sure."

"A recruiter? That's not how a proper lawyer finds a job," John said.

"It's not 1980 anymore. Things have changed, and that includes recruitment. Of course, I can always just leave you to your own devices, because that's worked so well for you so far."

"You're right," John said with a sigh. "Thank you. I do appreciate it."

"Good. You should. Because we could just dump you in front of your house right now and decide that's good enough. There's nothing saying we have to help you. But we will, because we're nice people that way," Rosie said.

I was glad Rosie was willing to do that for John. I knew what it felt like to be lost, not knowing what to do with your life while the world felt like it was moving on without you and everyone you knew seemed to have it all figured out. I'd felt that way myself until just a few short months ago.

We eventually pulled up to the house in Kula. If it wasn't for the fact that I knew this guy was one step away from bankruptcy, I would have been jealous as anything.

The huge house, painted navy blue, looked out over

the Pacific Ocean in the distance. The front of the house was lined with windows to take advantage of the incredible view. Three steps led up to an enormous covered lanai at the front, complete with plenty of lounging furniture to enjoy the sun setting with a glass of wine at the end of a long day.

Was Vanessa going to take John back, or was this all going to blow up spectacularly in my face?

Only one way to find out.

I knocked on the white door and waited.

About fifteen seconds passed before I heard the shuffling of feet heading toward the door. A moment later the lock clicked, and it swung open.

Vanessa didn't look nearly as well put together as she had the other day in the shop. Instead of the impeccably dressed woman I'd met only a couple of days earlier, I was now faced with a woman who looked more like a stay-at-home-mom with eighteen kids to take care of who had completely and totally lost it.

Vanessa's pajama bottoms were stained, and the T-shirt she wore was crumpled. Her eyes had bags beneath them, and her hair was no longer perfectly coiffed, but rather stuck out in every which direction.

As soon as she answered the door, her eyes fell on me, a mixture of hope and fear inside of them. A second later, though, they moved past me and landed on her husband.

"John!" Vanessa's voice was barely more than a hushed whisper, but the relief in her voice was palpable. Without hesitating for a second she rushed forward and wrapped her arms around him, burying her face in his shoulder while he hugged her awkwardly, obviously worried about her reaction to the news he was going to have to deliver to her.

"I love you," John murmured into her ear.

"Where were you? What happened?" Vanessa asked, not pulling away from her husband. John gently pried her away from him.

"I'll tell you everything, Ness, but before I do, I want you to know that everything I did was because I love you. Okay?"

Confusion passed over Vanessa's face. "Of course. Come on. Come inside, all of you. Please. I want to know how you brought my husband back to me."

She opened the door and let us all in, and I introduced Dot and Rosie as my associates. Vanessa pulled me aside and squeezed my arm in thanks. "I don't know how you found him, but thank you. You have no idea what this means to me. I was truly starting to lose hope that John would ever be found alive, especially after his car was..."

Vanessa broke away mid-sentence and swallowed hard, turning her head away to hide her tears.

"Look," I started awkwardly. Dealing with people's emotions was not my strong suit, but I was going to have to do my best here. "John is going to tell you what's been going on, and it's going to be hard for you to hear. So, uh, maybe prepare yourself for that as best you can."

"What do you mean?" Vanessa asked, her eyes widening slightly.

"It's better if John tells you himself. Come on. You deserve to know everything."

Two minutes later we were all seated in the expansive living room. The huge open space was made to look even larger with exposed wood beams in the A-frame ceiling. The walls were painted a light-sage color that contrasted beautifully against the exposed wood, and the couches were sleek black leather and comfortable. In front of us was an enormous live-edge coffee table.

"Tell me what happened, John," Vanessa begged. "Charlie says you have something to tell me."

John glanced over at me and swallowed hard. This was more awkward than the time I came back home from a party, cooked a giant plate of snacks, and opened my roommate's door asking, "Who wants bagel bites?" only to find him with a girl naked on top of him in the bed. I ended up just putting them on his dresser and going "I'll just leave these here for when you're done," and scurrying out of there as fast as I could.

Okay, maybe sitting here and listening to John admit to his wife that he'd been fired six months ago and had been lying to her ever since wasn't *quite* as bad as the bagel bites incident. But it was up there. And there was no way any of us were leaving and trusting John to actually tell Vanessa this on his own.

"Look," he said to Vanessa. "I want you to know that first of all, I screwed up. Badly. But I'm going to make it up to you."

Vanessa's eyes welled with tears, and when she spoke, her voice rose an octave. "You were with another woman, weren't you? You were gearing up to leave me."

"What? No, oh shoot, no, Vanessa. It's nothing like that," John replied hurriedly, reaching over and taking his wife's hands in his. "I swear, nothing like that has ever happened. I vowed to always be faithful to you, and I kept that vow. No, what I did was… different."

He paused, and the room was so quiet you could have heard a pin drop. Then, he told Vanessa everything. I had to admit, I'd expected John to try to gloss over some of the details, maybe make his midlife crisis out to be slightly less psychotic than it ended up being. But no, he told her everything. He told her how he was too humiliated to ask his peers for a job, and didn't know how to go about it. How he had faked his own death by leaving his car at the top of Haleakala and hitching a ride back down to the valley. He told her about his plan to flee to Mexico and start a new life with a new identity, leaving her with ten million dollars from his life insurance policy once he was declared dead, lost to the mountain.

By the time he was finished, both John and Vanessa were in tears.

"Why wouldn't you just tell me?" Vanessa asked, her voice cracking. "I could have taken it, John. I love you. I've always loved you. I never loved your job—I loved the man you were."

"I was too ashamed," John whispered. "I always wanted to provide for you. I wanted to be the best man you've ever met in your whole life. I wanted to give you everything you ever wanted, and when I was laid off, I realized I couldn't anymore, and I just couldn't handle it. I was worried you'd leave me. That you'd find someone else, someone who could hold a job."

Vanessa barked out a humorless laugh. "What kind of wife would that make me? Of course I appreciate that you worked while I raised our daughter. It was wonderful of you to do so much so that we could have this life. But that doesn't mean I was going to leave you if it all went away. I'd rather be homeless with you than live in a castle by myself, John. I can't believe you didn't see that."

"I… I wasn't thinking," John admitted. "I'm sorry, Ness. Please, forgive me. It doesn't have to be now. I know I have a lot to make up for. But just… please, don't leave. Not right away. Give me a chance."

"Oh, John. I'm not going to leave you. We've been through so much together. What kind of wife would I be if I gave up on you right now? It's not like you cheated. I know you did what you thought was best. You were wrong. So, so wrong. But you're here. And as long as we're together, I'm happy. We can do this. We'll find you another job. I know people too. I'll reach out to my network of moms. I'm sure we'll find you something."

John and Vanessa embraced right there on the couch, and I stood up, with Dot and Rosie doing the same. We had done our job. I'd found Vanessa's missing husband and brought him back to her. And it looked like there was going to be a happy ending for them after all.

In fact, the way they were on the couch right now,

there was probably a happy ending coming sooner rather than later.

"We're going to go," I said quietly, and the three of us exited via the front door.

"Wait!" Vanessa called out when we were halfway back to Queenie. She ran up to me. "I still owe you for what you did for us. As it turns out, um, I might not have as much money as I thought to pay you right now. But listen, invoice me, and let me talk to John, and we'll figure it out, okay?"

"Sure. We can sort out a payment plan of some sort," I said. "Rosie is going to help John find a new job as well, so maybe we can defer payment until then."

Vanessa's shoulders dropped in relief. "Thank you so much, Charlie. If there's anything I can ever do to repay you, please let me know. I almost lost John forever, and I would have if it weren't for you. I don't know what I would have done if I thought he was dead. Thank you. Not only for finding him, but for not letting him go through with this."

She turned to face Dot and Rosie. "Thank you to all three of you. There are no words to express how grateful I am."

"Go, be with your husband," Rosie said. "I'm sure the two of you have a lot to talk about. I'll be in touch with him soon about working with a recruiter."

Vanessa shot us another grateful glance then turned and went back into the house.

As we got back onto the road, I couldn't stop grinning. "We did good, ladies."

"Yes. We most certainly did," Rosie replied.

Chapter 22

I was meeting Bill Jamieson in his hotel suite at four o'clock that afternoon. He wasn't staying in the Maui Diamond, but rather at the Fairmont just a couple of buildings further along the beach. I headed up to his suite, on one of the upper floors, and knocked on the door. The man himself answered a moment later.

Bill Jamieson was taller in person than I'd expected. He stood about six foot two, and he was slim without being athletic. Had the person who attacked me been that tall? It was certainly possible. I wasn't one hundred percent sure; it had all happened so fast. He carried himself with the confidence that I assumed was inherent when you were a rich, older white man. And I had to admit, he was handsome. I mean, sure, he wasn't Jason Momoa hot, but who was?

"You must be Charlie," Bill said warmly, holding out a hand for me to shake. His grip was firm, and he motioned for me to enter the suite. "Please, come in. Anna says you're working for Marion to try to find out who killed that yoga instructor of hers. I'm not sure how I can help you, but I'll do whatever I can."

"Thanks," I replied, looking around. Bill was obviously the only person in the suite, and I was keenly aware of the fact that I was going to interview a potential murderer here, alone. I'd have to try actually thinking before I spoke, because if he was the killer, and he figured I was onto him, there was a very real chance I wouldn't make it out of this suite alive.

I very briefly questioned my choice of career.

"Can I get you anything?" Bill asked as he made his way to the kitchen. "I've got water, beer, spirits, Coke?"

"I'm good, thanks," I said, taking a seat in an armchair next to a very fragile-looking vase. I figured at least this way if Bill came at me, I could hurl it at his face as I ran out of the place.

"So, what crazy story has my ex-wife told you that's now affecting my life?" Bill asked as he poured himself a drink and took the couch across from me. He casually draped one arm over the back and rested one ankle on his opposite knee. Bill couldn't have looked more relaxed if he tried.

"What makes you think Marion has sent me after you?" I asked.

Bill laughed good-naturedly. "It's not my first time dealing with the consequences of having been married to that nutjob. Marion decides to go crazy and blame me for things, like poisoning that yoga instructor of hers, like I would have anything to do with that. But I understand you've got a job to do. It's the same thing I said to that police fella who stopped by here the other day. Yes, I was at the bar that night. No, I had nothing to do with that poor woman's death. Why would I? She was my ex-wife's yoga instructor, after all. But then, Marion was always good at turning things back around to herself. She thinks she was the intended victim, doesn't she? That would be like her. Can't let anybody else have the spotlight for even a moment. Everything has to be about Marion Hennessey. So, let's play the same charade we've always played. Ask your questions, and I'll endeavor to prove to you that I'm not a murderer. I'm just a man, trying to live his life without his ex-wife doing her best to ruin it at every opportunity."

Nothing screams "reasonable guy" like going on a long rant about how your ex-wife is crazy.

"All right, well, let's just throw out the whole suitcase instead of trying to unpack all that," I started. Bill just laughed.

"Don't worry. I'm used to people thinking I'm the bad guy. Marion has spent years bad-mouthing me to the press. Did you know, in Ancient Rome, whenever a historian didn't like an emperor, he would make up all these stories about the guy's sex life and write them down? That way, everyone would think the emperor was a pervert, and his reputation would be shot. That's what Marion does. She invents these stories about how I date women who are thirty years younger than me, how I date men, blah, blah, blah. Honestly, I don't even keep up with it anymore. What's the point? The people who really know me are aware that they're all lies, and the people who don't? Well, what do I care what Johnny Hillbilly in Buttfuck, Kentucky, thinks? Nothing, that's what. As long as he continues to see my movies, and of course he's going to. Nobody cares who the producer is. The only reason my name is ever in the news at all is because of who I married."

Right. It was time to ask this guy an actual question before he went on another long rant about how his ex was a nutjob who was just out to get him. "What took you to that particular bar that night?"

"I've heard good things about it. It was recommended to me by someone I met here in Hawaii, and I had the night off, so I figured why not check it out?"

"Did you make a reservation, or were you just a walk-in?"

Bill's eyes twinkled slightly, like he was expecting the question. "I asked Anna to make me a reservation earlier in the day. After all, I know the Maui Diamond is a busy resort, and I didn't want to have to wait for a spot at the bar."

"Did you know Marion was going to be there that night?"

"Believe it or not, Marion doesn't keep me appraised of her every move."

"Is that a no?" Bill's overly casual manner was starting to grate on me.

"That's a no. I didn't even know Marion was on the island."

"What are you doing here?"

"Working holiday. I'm producing a movie with

Rowan McLeod. I know some producers like to just throw money at a project and wipe their hands of it, but that's not me. I'm not micromanaging the director or anything like that, but I like to know what I'm working with. Sometimes, you can get a feel for whether a movie is going to be a total disaster based on how filming goes. If the main actors hate each other, for instance, sometimes it shows up in the final result. Sometimes it doesn't. But it helps to know about potential pitfalls ahead of time, so I'm here during filming."

"And how's it going so far? Are you in line to make another million dollars?"

Bill barked out a laugh. "I don't get out of bed for a movie that won't make me at least ten. So far, so good. It's looking good. And it should be, given the amount of money we've poured into it, and the stars attached to the movie. Have you met Rowan McLeod yet? He's the kind of man women can't resist."

"I have," I said. "He seems nice."

Bill shot me a salacious grin. "That's right. You're the woman in the photo making out with Rowan that's been making the rounds, aren't you?"

I could have denied it, but what was the point of that? My face was doing a pretty good job imitating a tomato either way."

"The general public has never been interested in where I put my mouth before, so I'm not exactly used to this whole thing," I said with a shrug.

"I'm not sure anyone ever gets *used* to it. It's like being a zoo animal, only there's no cages between you and the people who spend their days gawking at you.

And I never got it nearly as bad as Marion did. These days, the paparazzi only take pictures of me while I'm driving home and they're bored, waiting for Selena Gomez. She lives next door to me. But when I was married to Marion, it was constant and relentless. It was a nightmare."

"Well, speaking of cameras, one of them caught you talking to one of the waitresses on her way to the table serving Marion's group. Why did you stop her?"

Bill shrugged. "I haven't got a clue. The other cop asked me the same thing, and I gave him the same answer: why would I remember what I said to some random waitress at a bar a few days ago? I barely remember what I had for breakfast this morning."

"Did you know the drinks on her tray were headed to Marion's table?"

"You've got to be kidding. Of course not. How would I possibly know that?"

I shrugged. "Marion ordered a pina colada. Was that her regular drink?"

"Sure. But I'd also be willing to bet Marion wasn't the only person in the busy bar to order one. I mean, come on."

"You could have asked the waitress if that tray was destined for Marion's table," I suggested.

"I could have, but I most certainly didn't. As I said, I had no idea Marion was even on the island. I didn't know those drinks were headed to her table, and I certainly didn't poison one of them. You're doing some real straw clutching to make me out as a suspect here."

I hated to admit it, but Bill was right. If he hadn't

asked the waitress where those drinks were going, then how could he have known they were for Marion's table? It would have been one hell of a gamble, poisoning a drink that might have been for someone else. After all, Bill was also right that a pina colada wasn't exactly a rare drink order, especially on Maui.

"Okay," I said, switching tactics. "Let's say I believe you. You're just an innocent ex-husband who happened to be at the bar at the same time as someone tried to poison his ex-wife. Who do you think might have wanted her dead?"

Bill chuckled, but there was no humor behind the sound. "I imagine there are probably a few people out there who fit the bill. As to who would actually go ahead and do it? I have no idea. I'm not in her life anymore. She might leak untruths to the media to spoil my name, but the thing is, I haven't spoken to my ex-wife in at least six months. I don't know what she's up to at any given day. I don't care. And so no, I don't know who in her life would want her dead."

"Have you ever heard Rowan speak about her?" My heart clenched in my chest slightly as I mentioned his name in the context of being a murder suspect. I was almost certain Rowan was innocent, but I had to investigate all the same.

"No. We've never mentioned her. And I've spoken to the man a few times. If he had something against Marion, he would have told me. And I'm not just saying that because I don't want the bad press that would come from him getting nailed for attempted murder."

"Do you know Aaron Lewis, the yoga instructor?"

Bill let out a snort. "That one I *do* know. I tell you what, that man is a grifter through and through. I'm from LA, I can spot that crap from a mile away, and Lewis does not hide it well at all."

"How did you meet him?" I asked out of curiosity.

"He came to the set when we first started filming, a couple of weeks ago. He managed to talk his way past security, but I was a little bit harder to get rid of. He didn't tell me this, but he was looking for Rihanna, probably trying to add her to his client list. Everything about the man screamed slimy. He obviously doesn't care about yoga. He's just willing to use is as a vehicle to make as much money as possible."

"I agree with you there. And yet, Marion did see him for months."

"I imagine he appealed to her ego. But she must have eventually seen through him. For all her faults, Marion isn't an idiot. She's actually extremely intelligent. But when you're surrounded by fake people all day, every day, it can be hard to know who's actively harmful and who's just a grifter trying to get ahead by being someone they aren't."

"Do you think Aaron Lewis could have killed Marion?"

Bill looked at his glass carefully, tilted it toward him, and downed the rest in a single gulp, leaning his head back to do so. Then he looked at me for a moment before answering. "I think Aaron Lewis is the kind of man who would do anything that got him closer to his goals, whatever that might be. I think he's a psychopath. So the short answer to your question is yes. I think he could have done it."

"Am I going to walk down to the beach and listen to *My Favorite Murder* and have a story about him pop up one day?"

"It wouldn't surprise me. Have you met the guy?"

"Yes. And I think your assessment is disturbingly accurate."

"Well, there you have it. As much as TV shows and movies like to be complex, real life is usually much more simple. If you ask me, you've found someone in the circle who would be able to kill someone. Find a motive, and you've got yourself your guy."

I shot Bill a wry smile. "Have a lot of experience with murder investigations, do you?"

"No, but I understand human psyche. You can't make money in this industry if you don't. People believe what they see in the movies and on TV because they don't have any experience with it themselves, so they don't have any other frame of reference. But reality is very different to what the movie industry pretends reality to be. In any movie, Aaron Lewis would be the perfect red herring. But this isn't a movie, it's real life. Odds are he's your killer. What are the chances that there were two psychopaths at that table?"

What Bill didn't know was that I already had a motive for Aaron. He was angry that Marion had moved on and was seeing another yoga instructor. It was going to cost him money, maybe potential clients. After all, being able to brag that one of the most famous actresses in the world, a woman who exuded elegance and radiated beauty, took yoga lessons from *him* had to be better marketing than any paid advertising.

Bill grinned and put his feet up on the glass coffee table that sat between us. "There you go. See, I told you I had nothing to do with this. Now, can I be left in peace, or am I going to find myself dealing with more people knocking at my door and asking me the same questions?"

That was my cue. "Thanks for the help." I rose from my seat and headed to the front door.

"No problem. Sorry you had to waste your time. If I'd known going to that bar would have been so much trouble, I never would have bothered. I like a good drink, but not *this* badly."

"Did they live up to the hype? The drinks, I mean."

Bill shrugged. "They weren't bad, but they weren't life-changing. A bit overpriced, I think, but then everything in Wailea is overpriced."

"Good to know," I said, then with a goodbye nod I headed back out into the hallway and toward the elevators, running over the conversation we'd just had in my mind.

Nothing Bill Jamieson had said convinced me he was the killer. In fact, quite the opposite. He was right: it was all too much of a coincidence. Still, there was one part of his story I knew could be corroborated.

Chapter 23

I walked from the Fairmont to the Maui Diamond Resort, where I soon found myself at the Beachside Bar and Restaurant, where Bill had been sitting the night in question, and where Crystal had been killed.

Behind the bar, a young Asian man moved with the dexterity of someone who had been doing this a while, simultaneously taking orders, making drinks and keeping up a conversation with one of his regulars. He wore a black short-sleeved collared shirt, with a white vest over it, along with a pink bow tie with white polka dots. That was about as fancy as bartenders got on Maui. His black hair was short-cropped, a rainbow pin on his lapel added a splash of color, and on his wrist was a tattoo of the Grim Reaper sitting on a couch eating a plate full of cookies.

"Hi there," he greeted me as I slipped onto one of the stools. "What can I get started for you?"

"Mai tai, please." I pulled out my phone and

scrolled through my photos until I found the one I wanted. It was a picture Dot had sent of Bill Jamieson talking to the waitress. When the bartender returned, sliding my drink across the table to me, I flashed him my phone. "This woman wouldn't happen to be working tonight, would she? I'm investigating the murder of Marion Hennessey's yoga instructor."

The bartender's eyes flickered to the side for a split second before he answered. "I'm afraid I don't think she's on today."

"I don't think she's a suspect or anything," I said hurriedly, realizing he wasn't about to throw one of his coworkers under the bus. "But the guy she's talking to in this photo is, and I want to confirm with her what he stopped her about."

The bartender still didn't look a hundred percent convinced, so I figured I'd go for the full offensive. "Look, you're in this video, too, so I know you were working here that night. You're probably the person who made those drinks. If the real killer isn't found, tongues are going to start to wag, because this is Maui and it's a small island, and people are going to start throwing names out there. I know you don't want yours to be one of them, but it's going to be, since you made those drinks. So, why don't you help me find the person who actually did this, and you won't be known as the bartender whose drinks poisoned Marion Hennessey's yoga instructor."

That seemed to push him over the line. "All right, yeah. Fair enough. She's here. I'll go get her, but you have to talk to her here at the bar, and if I get any impression that you're threatening her, or implying that she's the one who killed that poor woman, I'll have security show you out. I take the safety of staff here very seriously."

"Understood," I replied. The man gave me a curt nod and headed off. I took a sip of my mai tai, one of the most popular drinks on the island. Half the bars and restaurants on Maui had their own version of the drink, which they often called a Maui tai, or some sort of similar play on words.

About two minutes later, the bartender returned, and behind him was the woman from the video. Tall and slim, with blond hair tied back in a low ponytail that reached halfway down her back, she looked at me, polite but cool. "Jazz here says you wanted to speak with me about the night that woman was killed?"

"Yes," I said, pulling out my phone and showing her the photo of Bill Jamieson. "When you had the tray of drinks that went to the table in question, this man stopped you and asked a question. Do you remember what that was?"

The woman squinted at the photo, frowning slightly as she tried to remember. About five seconds later, she nodded slowly. "Yes, I remember. I didn't think anything of it at the time, of course. After all, what with that poor woman dying and everything, I didn't give a second thought to anyone else. But he just wanted to know where the bathroom was."

"Oh. Is that it?"

"Yeah. He's another one of those Hollywood types, isn't he?"

"Why do you say that?"

"Everyone else in this restaurant was looking at the table where Marion Hennessey was sitting. But this guy, he didn't seem to care at all. In my experience, when we get celebrities, the only people who don't care are the types who work with them every day. Even foreigners who don't have a clue who they're looking at usually figure out what's going on and have a look. Of course, in this case, when we're talking about Marion, even the people at table seven that I was serving that night, who were from Japan, knew who she was. So did the people at table nine, from Denmark."

"Okay, cool, thanks," I said with a smile. "I appreciate the help."

"Not a problem." The woman looked like she was going to walk away, but then she paused.

"Is there anything else you want to tell me about that night?" I asked. "It doesn't matter if you don't think it was important."

"I'm sure it's nothing," the server said, looking around furtively, as if someone might be listening in. I didn't think there was too much of a risk of that; the stool to my left was empty, and to my right was a man who was so engrossed in the conversation he was having, I was pretty sure a nuclear bomb could go off without him noticing. Jazz the bartender was doing a good job of not floating over the server's shoulder, but I could tell he was subtly listening, making sure I wasn't harassing one of his coworkers. "But the thing is, I heard the yoga instructor was poisoned with Botox."

"She was," I confirmed.

"One of the men who was there, I've seen him before. He comes in fairly regularly. About two weeks earlier, I heard him on the phone speaking with someone about getting Botox injections."

I pulled out my phone and quickly did another Google search for Aaron's name. I held up the phone when I saw the photo of him. "This guy?"

The waitress nodded. "That's him. I don't want to get him in trouble if he didn't do anything."

"Don't worry. You did the right thing in telling me. I'm not going after someone if they didn't actually do this, but it's good to know."

The server gave me a small smile. "I hope you're successful. This is actually my first night back working since that night. I couldn't bring myself to come back here. That poor woman. She was so polite. Not everybody is, but she treated me like an actual human being. And to think, it was a drink that I brought to her that was poisoned. It's unbelievable."

The waitress shook her head sadly. I thanked her again for her time then sipped on my drink, nibbling on the straw a little as I thought about what I'd just learned.

"Get what you needed?" Jazz asked a moment later.

"Yeah. I'm afraid my good suspect just became far less good," I said with a small smile.

"Well, it happens. I'll give you the advice I always see in the movies: it's the last person you expect," Jazz said with a wink.

I laughed. "I wish it were that easy. Your Honor, I'd

like to submit every episode of CSI: Miami as evidence that proves this guy did it."

Jazz chuckled. "I think it's a good thing we're not in charge of this stuff. So, if you're investigating this murder, how close are you to finding the killer? If that's the sort of thing I can ask."

"Sorry," I said with a grin. There was a bit of irony to someone asking me that question when I put it to Jake so often. "Gotta keep the cards close to the chest. If there's one thing I've learned in this investigation, it's that literally everybody on the planet knows who Marion is and wants to know everything about her life."

"No kidding. People go nuts for celebrities in here. I wouldn't be able to live that way. She's had to send her bodyguards down to the beach to look for paparazzi before she goes for a dip in the pool, did you know that? I couldn't believe it. I didn't realize there even *were* any on Maui. This was ages ago, when she first started staying here. Now, I'm more used to it. But I couldn't do it myself. It looks like she lives in a bubble. No freedom at all. It sounds like the worst thing in the world to me." Jazz shook his head.

"I agree with you. My photo was on TMZ the other day, and it was awful."

Jazz grinned. "I saw that. It's why I didn't ask you for ID. Half the people on the planet know you're investigating this case now."

"That's not especially helpful."

"Well, the truth isn't always fun."

"You're not wrong."

Jazz was called down to the other end of the bar, and I continued working on my drink while I thought about the case. Eventually, I pulled out my phone and texted Dot.

Are you and Rosie up for drinks tonight, or is it too late for you?

Her reply came through a moment later. *That had better not be you implying we're old.*

I would never dream of it.

Where are you?

Maui Diamond. Following up to confirm something Bill Jamieson told me. I was thinking we could chat about the case. I think the kitchen is open for another hour if you haven't eaten yet. My treat.

You know I'm always up for free food. Okay, I'll be there soon. I'll text Rosie and pick her up on the way.

I grinned and put my phone away, then flagged down Jazz.

"Hey, mind if I move to one of the tables?"

"Sure," he said with a shrug. "Whichever empty one tickles your fancy is fine. I'll let one of the servers know she's got an extra customer."

"Thanks," I said with a smile, holding up my glass. "I appreciate the help here tonight."

"You need anything else, you let me know, okay?"

Chapter 24

I moved from the bar to one of the booths, in fact the same one where I'd had dinner with Rowan just the other night. I preferred the booths to the tables here; the tables were where I'd been kidnapped at gunpoint once.

A couple of minutes later, a server arrived, dropping off a menu and taking my order for a second mai tai. I casually perused the menu, my stomach grumbling at the thought of a Kahlua-pork-and-pineapple pizza. I placed my order when the server returned with the drink, and about five minutes later, Dot and Rosie slipped into the booth across from me. Dot was dressed entirely in a velour sweatsuit, while Rosie still looked as if she'd just come home from a day at the office. I was pretty sure she didn't know what "casual" meant.

"So, what did you find out from Bill Jamieson?" Rosie asked, while Dot snatched the menu and focused on the free food she was about to get.

I recounted the conversation I had with him and then explained how I'd confirmed his story about asking the waitress something unimportant.

"He wasn't lying, then," Dot said, proving she was listening to our conversation and not one hundred percent focused on deciding what burger she was about to devour. "I can tell from your voice, you don't think it's him."

"No," I admitted. "I thought he was a great suspect, but after speaking to the man, I think it's just a coincidence that he was at the bar at the exact same time as someone else tried to kill Marion. Especially after confirming that he just asked the waitress where the bathrooms were. No matter what, I keep coming back to this one fact: there's no way Bill could have known *that* tray was going to Marion's table, and it would take a special kind of psychopath to risk killing a random drinker of a pina colada on the off chance it was going to his ex-wife."

"That's an excellent point," Rosie said.

"Still, something in the conversation I've just had is nagging at me," I said, stirring my drink and listening to the ice cubes clink in the glass. I picked out the maraschino cherry and bit it off the stem, which I dropped onto a napkin. "I can't quite figure out what it is, though. It's like it's flittering right on the outskirts of my brain, and I'm trying to grab at it and find out what information I need, but it's just out of reach at all times."

"That's frustrating," Rosie said. "It will come to

you, though. Sometimes, trying to think about it incredibly hard only makes things worse."

"I know," I muttered. "But I want to know *now*. This is important. I can feel it in my bones. It might even be a key to breaking this whole case wide open, but I can't figure out what it is."

"Well, keep talking about this case, and see what drops out of that brain of yours," Dot said, putting down the menu. "Tonight feels like a cheeseburger kind of night. With onion rings."

"You always get a cheeseburger when we go out," Rosie said. "How is this different to any other night?"

"Exactly right, it isn't. And I only get cheeseburgers because they're so much better than anything else most restaurants have to offer."

"I ordered my pizza before you two got here. I was hungry," I said. As if right on cue, the server arrived with my food, and Rosie and Dot ordered theirs while I dug in.

"Since you ordered before we got here, I feel it's only fair that I get a slice of that pizza now," Dot said, eyeing my pie greedily.

I laughed. "Go for it, but I'm going to be demanding an onion ring in return when your food arrives."

"I accept your terms," Dot said, reaching across the table and grabbing a slice off my plate. I pushed it toward Rosie, raising my eyebrows slightly in question, silently asking if she wanted a slice.

"Thank you, but no. I'm content to wait for my order to arrive. But by all means, go ahead and start.

We can all see Dot has," Rosie said, shooting a smile at her friend, who had what appeared to be about half the slice of pizza shoved into her mouth.

Dot muttered something in Rosie's direction, but her mouth was so full I had no chance at figuring out exactly what it was.

I munched on a slice of pizza myself, trying to figure out what it was my brain wanted me to realize was an important clue. What was I missing from that last conversation?

Before I had a chance to think about it further, someone slinked into the booth next to me. It was Jake.

"Mind if I join you ladies?" he asked with a cheeky smile.

"As long as your partner isn't anywhere near here," Dot replied.

"No. He's off the clock. So am I, technically. But something about this case is bugging me, so I thought I'd come back here and see if I could get some inspiration. Or new information. You never know what someone doesn't know they know."

"So, did you find anything interesting? Or is that secret police information you can't tell us about?" I asked, rolling my eyes just slightly.

"You already know it's the latter," Jake said with an amused smile. "But I figured I can still come and spend some time with you. Although, isn't it a bit late for the two of you?" he said, looking at Dot and Rosie.

"Why would that be?" Dot asked, tilting her head to the side slightly in confusion.

"Well, people your age are usually in bed by now, or at least at home."

I choked on my drink.

"Excuse me?" Dot said, visibly annoyed. "Are you calling us old?"

"Definitely not," Jake said hurriedly, holding his hands in front of him in surrender. "Wouldn't dream of it."

"Good, because if you did, there'd be a second murder committed here in this restaurant tonight," Dot said, stroking the handle of the steak knife next to her while maintaining eye contact with Jake.

"You do realize you're threatening a police officer, right?" Jake asked, completely nonplussed as he raised a single eyebrow skyward.

"You do realize you called me old first, right?" Dot shot back.

"I'm starting to understand why you and Charlie are such good friends."

"Yeah, I'm on Dot's side," I said, taking another bite of pizza. "You call her old, you get what you get."

"That is not at all how the law works."

"It would if I were in charge."

"I for one am glad you aren't, although I do apologize for implying you're old. What are you young ladies doing here tonight?"

"That's better," Dot said, narrowing her eyes in his direction. "We're celebrating the successful closing of another case."

"I didn't realize you had another case."

"John Waters," I explained.

"The guy who got lost on Haleakala? I saw the missing person's file this morning. You mean he's not dead?"

I shook my head. "Faking it for the insurance money, because he was too scared to tell his wife they were broke."

"Huh. Go figure. That's not how I expected that one to end. But hey, I'd rather that be the outcome than having to tell his wife his body was found. How did she take the news?"

"About as well as can be expected, I guess. Personally, if a guy did that to me, I'd tell him to go take that hike on the volcano."

Jake chuckled. "I can't say I'd blame you. How did she not know he was broke?"

"Old-fashioned families," Rosie answered with a shake of the head. "I saw it all the time at the bank. Men who took care of all the household finances. They'd give the wife money to buy groceries and maybe a little extra if they were lucky, but that was it. The women had no idea what the overall financial state of the household was. It was actually quite common until not that long ago."

"I'm glad things have changed for the better in that respect. But hopefully now John and Vanessa will make some changes that allow them both to know what's going on in their house, financially," I said.

I looked up then, and I spotted Rowan suddenly. He must have been walking across the restaurant. He stopped and looked at me, and I went to raise my hand up in greeting, when suddenly the server arrived with Dot and Rosie's food, blocking my view of him.

She placed the plates down and took a drink order from Jake, but by the time she'd left, Rowan was gone. I didn't think anything of it, and instead turned back to the table, where I yanked an onion ring off Dot's plate.

"I was promised this earlier," I said, chomping into the crispy batter.

"I've never been a fan of onion rings," Rosie said as she started on the margherita pizza she ordered. "I'm more of a French fry girl."

"That's because fries are the standard, and that's you. You're a completely normal American in every way," Dot said.

"You've got me there," Rosie said with a grin. "Although in this particular case, you're the one who's ordered a burger and rings, while I went for the Italian. Why didn't you order any food, Jake? You need to keep your energy up. My bet is you've had a long day and you need some sustenance. Besides, Charlie's buying."

"Hey, I said I was buying for you two," I said with a grin. "I didn't say anything about Jake."

"That's just Rosie trying to make you pay for his meal so she can pretend you're dating," Dot said with a mischievous chuckle, and I kicked at her under the table. Somehow, as if she knew what I was about to do, she'd gotten her leg out of the way in time and cackled with laughter as she felt my foot connect with the booth. "Too slow!"

I glared in her direction while studiously avoiding Jake's gaze.

"I wouldn't expect Charlie to pay for my meal, not when I'm the one who dropped in here uninvited. But I've already eaten dinner, so I'm all right. But thank you."

"Plus, when he's only ordered a drink, he gets to bail quickly when the two of you start acting like weird matchmakers," I added.

"Who? Me? Not a chance," Dot said, diving back into her burger while I resisted the urge to roll my eyes.

"All right, well in that case, why don't you tell us who you were here to see?" Rosie asked.

"Because this is an open police investigation and I can't talk about a case."

"Oh, come on. Who are we going to tell?" Dot said. "No one would believe us even if you did tell us who the killer is. Are you at least close to figuring out who it is?"

"I was going to ask you the same question."

"And you weren't going to get a response," Rosie said. "Not without giving us something first."

"Oh? Is that how you think this works?" Jake asked good-naturedly. "You really think you can hold out information from me longer than I can?"

"Are we taking bets here? Because I put literally all the money I have on Rosie," I said.

"Now, now. Don't be mean to the poor man. He doesn't realize what he'd be up against," Rosie said, shooting a wink in my direction.

Jake, of course, had no way of knowing that Rosie was a former KGB agent who had infiltrated the United States before defecting and starting a new life on Maui. He could have been the best police officer in the country and there was still no way he'd win against Rosie if the two went toe-to-toe in a battle of wills.

"All right, it's been a long day. How about we talk about something else?" Jake suggested with a smile. "Something that doesn't involve murder, or how Rosie would make a formidable opponent in a battle of wills?"

"Works for me. I prefer to keep my superpowers under wraps, anyway," Rosie said with a sly smile. "I'm sure we can find something else to talk about."

Chapter 25

About an hour later, we'd finished our meals, the conversation waned, and we eventually decided to all go our separate ways. It was nearly eight o'clock anyway, and I had a shift at Aloha Ice Cream in the morning. Then, I figured I was going to visit Aaron Lewis again, and see if I couldn't find proof he was the killer.

I had parked Queenie in the underground lot beneath the resort. I took the elevator down to P2 then began walking toward my Jeep. I felt a little bit of a buzz, but I'd only had two drinks, and it had been at least half an hour since I finished the last one, so I was good to drive home.

As I walked through the practically deserted garage, I suddenly realized what I had been trying to think of back in the restaurant. Everything clicked into place, and I realized I knew exactly who had killed Crystal.

I just had to prove it. I excitedly rushed toward

Queenie, thinking about nothing other than getting home and proving my theory before going to Jake and having the perpetrator arrested.

I had just gotten into the front seat when suddenly pain coursed through my body and I blacked out.

I BLINKED MY EYES OPEN, THE WORLD LOOKING woozy as I came to. What on earth had just happened? My right shoulder felt like it was on fire, and why did my whole body hurt?

"That's right," a voice next to me said. "Come to, nice and easy. You're going to drive out of here like nothing's happened, okay?"

My veins turned to ice. There was someone in the car with me. Cool. This was nothing to worry about. It was just how tons of people ended up murdered. I listened to *My Favorite Murder* regularly. I knew this was how it worked. And I also knew the most important thing I had to do right now was survive.

It was too bad my brain wasn't quite working at a hundred percent. I looked over to see my assailant. He had brown hair and looked familiar. "Aaron?" I muttered.

The person next to me laughed. "No. It's not Aaron, although that's what I want the security cameras to think."

When I heard Marion Hennessey's voice, everything came back to me. She was the killer. She had poisoned her own drink, knowing that Crystal wouldn't be able to drink hers, and offered to switch.

"Marion," I said slowly, trying to bring everything back into focus. Slowly, my eyes adjusted again, although the pain didn't dissipate. I looked down to see her holding a Taser only a few inches from me.

"That's right. And if you don't want to be electrocuted again, I highly recommend you do exactly as I tell you."

I groaned and leaned back in the seat. Of course I'd been Tasered. Again. But looking at Marion, she didn't look like Marion. Gone was the perfect hair and makeup. No, she was wearing makeup. But it was meant to make her look like someone else. So was the wig.

"You're pretending to be Aaron," I said. "You want the security cameras to catch me leaving this parking garage with him in my car."

"Very good," Marion said, her voice patronizing. "I need to pin this murder on someone. And obviously it can't be me. Now, drive."

The keys were already in the ignition, although I couldn't remember if I'd put them there before getting Tasered, or if Marion had done it while I was passed out. But I started the car and pulled out of the space.

"I figured out it was you, you know," I said. "I was about to go home and prove it. Then I was going to tell Jake everything."

"If only you were a bit faster on the draw," Marion said. "That's why I'm doing this. I was worried you were getting too close to the truth, and I couldn't have that."

"You're the one who poisoned the drink. You wanted people to see you as a victim. You've done a few subpar movies, and your reputation isn't what it once was. You wanted to be Marion Hennessey, matron of the silver screen. The most famous woman in the world. You wanted to be the Katharine Hepburn of the twenty-first century. You wanted to make Meryl Streep and Helen Mirren look like last year's news. But instead, everything seemed to be going against you. So, you decided to take charge of the situation yourself."

I pulled out from the resort and reached the road. "Take a left. Go north, toward Ka'anapali," Marion ordered. "And you're completely right. It's not fair. Do you know what they were calling me in the press? Washed up. A has-been. I am barely fifty years old. Do you know how much more I have left in me? I might not be playing twenty-year-olds anymore, but I deserve roles that are appropriate for a woman of my status. Roles like those taken by Judi Dench. But they're not being offered to me, and you know why? Because of these stupid slanderous reports. I made a couple of mistakes with roles I took on, and suddenly it's like I'm box office poison. Well, I'm reclaiming the narrative for myself."

"And you decided to do that by poisoning your yoga instructor and making yourself out to be the victim."

"People love a victim. Everyone feels sorry for the person who's had something done to them that wasn't their fault. It's the easiest way to get sympathy from the public. So having been there when my yoga instructor was murdered? That was a great start. The news reported that I jumped into action. It made me look like a hero."

"And then of course, you're the one who attacked me when I went to your suite. There was no assailant who had come after you. You knew I was coming, so you sent Amber away, and you dressed yourself up to look a bit bigger, then hit me over the head immediately."

"That's right. There were no cameras in the hallway, so I knew I'd get away with it. Then, I just had to drag you inside, change back into my regular clothes, and tell you what you saw. I knew you'd believe it."

"It all happened so fast I didn't realize it was you," I said. "But of course, it made perfect sense. There was no one else in the room. No sign of anyone else having been there. We all took it as the intruder being careful. Wearing gloves, and being sure not to leave any DNA. But the truth was simpler than that: there was no intruder. But it made all the papers that someone was really out there trying to kill you."

"I've had interviews with *People*, *Good Morning America*, *Entertainment Tonight,* and more requests than I could possibly fulfill," Marion purred, obviously pleased with herself. "My star is on the rise once more. I've just finished filming an artsy movie that will make no money but that critics will love. I'm putting my name back on the map."

"You're putting your name on a list of inmates at

Halawa," I said. "Do you really think you're going to get away with this?"

"Of course I do," Marion said with a scoff. "After all, I'm the victim here. Nobody ever suspects the victim. And after they find your body, the police are going to scour all the tapes and find video of you leaving with Aaron Lewis. Sure, my disguise isn't perfect, but it doesn't have to be. Security footage is notoriously awful. It'll look enough like him that that's the direction they'll all be looking. And if I'm lucky, he won't take a deal. He'll think he'll be let off, because he's actually innocent. And then I'll get to testify at his trial. Oh, there will be so much attention around it. So many opportunities for me to look like the stoic woman doing a difficult thing to get justice."

Cool, the woman who hired me was actually an insane psychopath. Why couldn't I have figured out she was the killer, like, I don't know, five minutes earlier? Then I could have told Jake, and he could have come with me to the car, and he probably would have realized there was someone hiding in the back seat waiting to Taser me.

No, I couldn't think about that. Right now, my priority had to be to survive. The past was done and dusted. What could I do going forward that meant I'd get out of here alive? Because there was no way Marion intended to let me walk away from here.

"So, what happens now?" I asked. "Where are we driving to?"

"I'll tell you when we get there. Just keep driving toward Ka'anapali."

I glanced down at the Taser, which Marion kept only a few centimeters from my side. If I did anything she didn't like, I was done for.

"Bill had nothing to do with any of this, did he?" I asked, just to be sure.

Marion barked out a laugh. "That idiot? No, of course not. Although I have to admit, I did consider pinning it on him when I found out he was there that night. He would have deserved it. He's always telling everyone how crazy I am, when they don't realize he was the worst husband ever."

"Yeah, you're just a picture of sanity right now," I mumbled under my breath.

"Be careful," Marion warned. "I'm not afraid to use this. Eyes on the road. Keep driving."

I continued on, my mind whirring. I couldn't see a way out of this. The best-case scenario was mutually assured destruction. If I did something, Marion would Taser me again, and the car would likely crash. There was a chance we would both die, and that was basically the best-case scenario I had right now.

It wasn't exactly ideal.

Coming out of Kihei, I turned left at the highway intersection that led toward West Maui. It was late, which meant traffic was light.

What would Rosie or Dot do? They were much better than me in situations like this. Should I just keep driving and then hope that when we got out of the car, I'd be able to overpower Marion?

No, right now, I was in charge of a two-ton Jeep.

This was as in control of the situation as I was ever going to be.

Then, I realized what they would do. How did you deal with a psychopath? You had to out-psycho them. The most important thing to Marion was her ego and her reputation. My best chance to get out of this was to ruin that. Mutually assured destruction it was.

I pressed on the gas, and Queenie lurched forward as the speedometer shot to the right on the dashboard.

"What are you doing?" Marion asked, looking around. I didn't answer her. Instead, I pressed on the gas even more. Olivia had done good work on this vehicle, and the Jeep barely groaned as it sped up from forty, to fifty, to sixty.

"Slow down," Marion ordered, but instead I drove the car faster. "What are you doing?"

I turned to look at her. "If we crash, they'll find both our bodies in the wreckage. You're dressed like someone else. The police will put two and two together. You'll go down in history as a murderer. People will speak your name in the same sentence as they do O.J. Simpson. Are you really prepared for that? I'm ready to die tonight, Marion. Are you?"

The speedometer raced past seventy miles an hour. The road along here was slightly twisty. I wasn't losing control of the car in the corners just yet, but the G forces were starting to get pretty strong, and the tires squealed against the concrete as they tried to keep a grip.

"Slow down," Marion said. "Slow down right now, or I'm going to Taser you."

"Again, you do that, and we both die. Are you really prepared to die today, Marion? Is this the legacy you want to leave? A killer, dead on Maui while trying to frame someone else for the murder you committed?"

I really, really was not prepared to die, and I was bluffing my ass off. But I had a feeling neither was Marion. This was the most terrifying game of chicken I'd ever played, and I really needed to come out ahead.

There was a car in front of me, and I had to swerve into the oncoming traffic lane to avoid it. Queenie tipped perilously to the side as I did so but righted herself just in time. Marion clutched the side of the car, dropping the Taser as she did so. It was then that I realized she wasn't wearing a seat belt.

This was my chance.

I slammed on the brakes as hard as I could. The tires screeched underneath as the car slid to the right slightly. The air was forced out of my lungs as I was pressed against the seat belt, my head whipping forward, and I closed my eyes and gritted my teeth against the pressure of the deceleration.

There was a thud on the other side of the car as Marion's body was propelled forward and into the dashboard and the windshield.

"Always wear your seat belt," I said, breathing heavily from the adrenaline. Marion was crumpled in a ball on the floor of the car, and I could just see the Taser sticking out from under her. I reached over and grabbed it, then threw it out the window. I wasn't about to risk getting Tasered twice in one night.

It was about ten miles to the closest police station,

up past Lahaina. Normally, with just a little traffic, it was about a fifteen-minute drive. But given the time of night, and the adrenaline coursing through my body, I made it in under ten. Marion never moved from the spot on the floor of the Jeep, crumpled in place and groaning. I figured there was a good chance she had some internal bleeding or something, but I wasn't especially inclined to save her.

When I reached the police station I explained to them who I was, asked them to call Jake for me—I had no idea where my phone was, but I knew it was long gone—and then settled in as the magnitude of the night hit me like a truck.

Chapter 26

"I can't believe I patched up a guy with third-degree burns who wanted to get a cool video for Instagram and went surfing after setting his board on fire, and somehow *you* still had the more exciting night," Zoe said when I got home, a couple hours later. She'd just arrived home from her shift at the hospital. I told her everything that had happened. "You really should get checked out if you've been Tasered again."

"I'm fine, really," I said with a wave of my hand. "I'm starting to get used to it."

"You must realize how insane that sounds."

"Cut me a bit of slack; I got Tasered last night."

"Marion's in jail then? And she survived?"

I nodded. "As far as I know. I think they took her to the hospital, though. Who knows, maybe you'll get to take care of her."

"I hope not. As much as I would, since it's my duty, I don't want to ease the pain of someone who tried to kill my best friend. I'm glad my shift ended before she was brought in."

"I don't think anyone would mind if you snuck into her room and changed her chart so she got fewer pain meds."

Zoe snorted. "Yeah, I'm sure I wouldn't get into trouble for that at all."

"Well, it was worth suggesting."

"I can't believe she killed one person and tried to kill a second just for her career. I mean, I'm as ambitious as anybody, and I'd never do that."

"That's because you're not an insane psychopath," I replied. "I should have picked it up earlier. A few people mentioned to me that Marion really let the fame get to her head. Having her name in the papers and all that. And Bill Jamieson told me his ex-wife was nuts. But I mean, lots of dudes say that about their exes. It's a giant red flag, and that was what I took it as when Bill said it to me. But it turned out he was actually right. He wasn't exaggerating or trying to play the victim. She's a straight-up psycho."

"That one's not on you. Normally when a guy complains about his ex being crazy, that's a him problem, not a her problem."

"True," I said. "Anyway, I want to know more about this guy who set himself on fire while surfing. There has to be more to the story than that."

Zoe laughed. "Let me just say, if you're ever going to go surfing, try not to set yourself on fire. Also, he's very lucky the water was literally right there."

"What did he do?"

"He had a friend go out with him. He poured paint thinner along the edge of his board. The plan was to set it alight right as he was catching a wave, and then his friend would take pictures of him as he rode the wave with the flames shooting up from the board."

"Honestly, that sounds super badass."

Zoe laughed. "It might have been, if it weren't for the fact that the idiot managed to pour some of the lighter fluid on his own skin without realizing it. He set the board on fire, and lo and behold, his leg went up in flames too."

I cringed. "This is why women live longer than men. So he showed up in your ER?"

"Yeah, just after seven. Third degree burns to his right leg. He's not going to be surfing for a little while."

"And hopefully when he does, he'll leave the paint thinner at home."

"No kidding. I think the guy's going to be scared of fire for life."

"It's still good to know somebody had a worse night than I did. And mine wasn't even my fault."

"For once. Have you spoken to Dot and Rosie?"

"Not yet. I don't know where my phone is, but I think it's probably long gone. Marion probably threw it away while I was passed out after being Tasered. Same with the rest of my purse, which is a bit annoying. Not the first time it's happened, though. I lost all my stuff a bunch of times back in the day, usually after a long night out. At least this time I've still got my dignity."

Zoe snorted. "That's something, I guess. Do you

want to drive down to the resort and see if we can find your things?"

"You must be exhausted."

"Yeah, but you must be too."

"I am," I admitted.

"Okay, look. You go to sleep. I'll go down to the resort and see if I can track down your stuff."

"I can't let you do that," I argued, but Zoe held up a hand.

"Doctor's orders. Go to bed, Charlie. It's not just that you had a big night physically. It's mental as well."

"So did you."

"I patched people up in the ER. I didn't get Tasered and then almost have to crash my car to save my own life. There's a difference. We're not discussing this. Go to bed. I'll let Dot and Rosie know what happened."

I had no choice but to relent. "Okay. Thanks, Zoe."

"Don't mention it. This is what friends are for. I'll see you when you wake up, okay?"

I headed into the bedroom, where Coco had taken the opportunity to spread herself out on far more of the bed than a dachshund-golden-retriever cross had any right to, and crawled under the covers.

Coco stirred and pressed herself against my leg, and we were both asleep within seconds.

I WOKE UP TO THE SOUND OF A KNOCK AT THE DOOR.

"I'm coming," I called out as I dragged myself out

of bed. I stifled a yawn as I headed to the front door and opened it to find Rowan McLeod standing there.

He raised an eyebrow when he saw me. "Long night?"

"Don't judge, someone tried to murder me," I said, opening the door to let him in. "I get a free pass for looking like I just came home from a bender."

Rowan chuckled as he entered the apartment. "Fair enough. I heard what happened. I just wanted to check and see that you're okay."

"I'm all good. Coffee?"

Rowan shook his head. "No, thanks."

Thankfully, Zoe had put a pot on at some point, so I poured myself a mug.

"What time is it?"

"Just after noon."

"Oh, shoot. I was supposed to work this morning," I said, my eyes widening. I didn't even have my phone to text Leslie. Hopefully she'd forgive me.

"It happens. As you said, someone tried to kill you. If your boss doesn't give you a day off for that, it's probably time to get a new job."

"That's a good point. Anyway, how did you hear about what happened?"

"Word got around set. I'm pretty sure it's on the internet by now too."

I groaned. "Great. That's just what I need. Is my photo on TMZ again?"

"Don't worry, I'm sure they're having a ball with Marion's mug shot. Someone leaked it about ten minutes ago. I got a text just as I was coming up here."

"How did you know where I live, anyway? Don't tell me I've got a stalker situation on my hands."

Rowan's mouth curved upward. "Nothing quite so nefarious. I was speaking to one of the extras on set a few days ago. She mentioned that she lived a couple doors down from you. When I left her, I found she'd snuck a pair of underwear into my pocket, along with an address."

I choked on the coffee I was drinking, coughing up half a lung while Rowan pounded on my back. "Now you know how surprised I was," he said with a laugh.

"Vesper actually did that?" I asked when I finally got control of myself, wiping a tear from my eye.

"She did. I almost came here in disguise so she wouldn't recognize me, and I snuck up the stairs holding my breath the entire time. I don't know what I would have done if she saw me."

I laughed. "I appreciate you putting your body on the line for me like that."

"Anytime. So, Marion really poisoned Crystal, hey?"

I nodded. "Yeah. All in a deluded attempt to make herself out to be a victim and have some good press written about her."

Rowan shook his head. "This industry. It can be tough, and it's not for everyone. Obviously it drove Marion over the edge."

"And then she almost had me drive over the edge of a cliff. Actually, I'm not sure what she planned, exactly. She wanted me to go toward Ka'anapali. There are a lot of good ways to dispose of a body up past there."

"Whatever she had in mind, I'm glad it failed. Do you know if she's talking to the cops?"

"I don't know. When I brought her in, she was pretty quickly whisked away, and as I was leaving I heard someone mention that they'd called for an ambulance. I guess if they got her mug shot, she must be okay enough to be discharged."

"Must be."

"Listen, how much longer are you on the island for? Because I know that Vesper propositioned you, but how about I offer to take you out to dinner instead? Move a little more slowly."

Rowan gave me a sad smile. "You have no idea how much I'd love to take you up on that offer. But I can't."

"Why? Am I not famous enough for you?" I teased.

"If you really think that would stop me, then you don't know me at all. No, I'm just not looking for something casual right now."

"Who says I am?"

"The look on your face whenever you look at that cop. I saw you with him last night, in the restaurant."

"Jake?" I asked, incredulous. "No, you've got it all wrong. I definitely don't have feelings for him. He's the most annoying, frustrating person I've ever met. He wasn't even invited yesterday. I was with Dot and Rosie, and he just showed up."

Rowan tilted his head to the side slightly. "I know what I saw. You might not be ready to accept it, but it's the truth. So no, I won't take you up on your offer, because as much as I like you, I also won't play second fiddle to someone else. But if one day you move on from Jake, and I happen to be here shooting something else, hit me up."

"I really, really do not like Jake that way," I spluttered, too surprised to say anything else.

"Keep telling yourself that," Rowan said gently. "I'm glad you're okay. I've got to get back to set."

He walked over toward me, so close I could feel the heat from his body and smell the aftershave emanating from him. I inhaled sharply, but when Rowan leaned in, he simply kissed me softly on the cheek.

"Take care, Charlie."

I stood there in the kitchen, stunned, as Rowan McLeod left my apartment.

I didn't have feelings for Jake. That was the most ridiculous thing I'd ever heard in my life.

Suddenly, I heard a voice from the hallway. "Found the gift I left in your pocket, did you?" It was Vesper, and I stifled a laugh. I headed to the lanai and looked out on the parking lot, where a moment later Rowan was sprinting back toward the Audi he'd driven up here in.

I chuckled to myself. Rowan was totally wrong about my feelings for Jake. There was nothing there, and there never would be.

Right?

Book 5 - Hibiscus Homicide - When a tourist is murdered in Ka'anapali, and it turns out he's someone from Rosie's past, Charlie is on the case. She needs to find out whether or not the man knew about Rosie's defection, or if it's just a coincidence he was killed on the island.

And while the stakes couldn't be higher, Charlie finds herself butting heads with the FBI, at the same time as she's getting closer to Jake than ever.

Charlie has to get to the bottom of this case before Rosie's true identity is revealed, but going up against trained spies is completely outside her wheelhouse.

Will Charlie find the killer and protect her friend, or is she going to find herself out in the cold… permanently?

Visit your storefront to pre-order your copy of Hibiscus Homicide now (coming July 26th, 2022)

About the Author

Jasmine Webb is a thirty-something who lives in the mountains most of the year, dreaming of the beach. When she's not writing stories you can find her chasing her old dog around, hiking up moderately-sized hills, or playing Pokemon Go.

Sign up for Jasmine's newsletter to be the first to find out about new releases here: http://www.authorjasminewebb.com/newsletter

You can also connect with her on other social media here:

Also by Jasmine Webb

Charlotte Gibson Mysteries

Aloha Alibi

Maui Murder

Beachside Bullet

Pina Colada Poison

Hibiscus Homicide (coming July 2022)

www.ingramcontent.com/pod-product-compliance
Lightning Source LLC
Chambersburg PA
CBHW030527310726
48979CB00010B/1835/J

* 9 7 8 1 7 7 7 7 9 9 3 3 5 *